First Kiss
Just A Little Crush

Elouise East

Copyright © 2019 Elouise East

FIRST KISS (JUST A LITTLE CRUSH, BOOK 1)

ALL RIGHTS RESERVED

No part of this book may be reproduced or transmitted in any form or by any means, electronic or mechanical including photocopying, recording, or by any information storage or retrieval system, without permission in writing from the publisher, Elouise East. No part of this book may be scanned, uploaded or distributed via the internet or by any other means, electronic or print, without premising from Elouise East.

The unauthorised reproduction or distribution of this copyrighted work is illegal. Please purchase only authorised electronic or print editions and do not participate in or encourage the electronic piracy of copyrighted material. Your support of the author's rights and livelihood is appreciated.

This is a work of fiction. Names, characters, places and incidents are either the product of the author's imagination or are used fictitiously and any resemblance to any actual persons, living or dead, events, or locales is entirely coincidental.

All products and/or brand names mentioned are registered trademarks of their respective holders/companies.

Publisher: Elouise East

Cover Design: Covers by Jo

Editor: Elouise East

Beta Readers: Courtney Green, Emma Brown

Contents

Dedication

For C, thank you from the bottom of my heart, you don't realise how much you helped.

For Lee, thank you for all your support and generosity through my journey.

For my family, who put up with all my crazy ideas.

Author Note

This book is taboo in nature. If this is something you prefer not to read, please go to https://elouiseeast.com/triggers to check the contents.

1

Charlie

"Yo, Charlie! Can we have beers all round when you get a sec?" shouted Johnson, one of his regulars, over the din in the bar. Charlie gave him a nod and a smile, continuing with his current order. As his body went on autopilot to fill the pint, he thought back to this morning and seeing Josh naked in the bathroom. He felt the flush heat his cheeks and distracted himself by looking around the bar. He nodded softly when he saw how busy it was.

In the six years since it had opened, Crush was considered by some a step above the other bars in Cambridge, making it a popular hangout. It had a good indoor space and the admittedly overgrown outdoor deck area had a view of the River Cam.

Crush catered to customers of all ages and walks of life. Currently, it was nearing five, and the busy period didn't usually start until six, but for some reason, there had been a huge rush of people within the last half hour—not that he was complaining.

Charlie finished pulling the pint and passed it over to the customer, receiving payment in return. He paid it into the till, returning the change and grabbing glasses for Johnson's order. If he'd seen correctly, another guy had joined their table, so he set five pints onto a tray.

"Gemma!" Charlie hollered to get the waitress's attention. "These are for Johnson. I counted five guys but let me know if that's wrong." He turned his attention to the bar, absently counting how many customers were trying to grab his eye. He blew out a breath. "I might have to call Analise in," he mumbled to himself as he grabbed a quick gulp of water and started on the next order.

He had been a bartender for the last year and loved every minute of it. He had known for years he wanted to work in a bar or restaurant environment. It must be in his blood—the atmosphere, the people he met, and the ebb and flow of the environment called to him. Luckily for him, as soon as he turned eighteen, a job had come up at Crush and he'd asked Tom, the manager, about it. And the rest, as they say, is history. He was on his way to a management role, with a couple more years' experience and Tom's tutelage. He knew he was young compared to other managers, but Charlie had worked hard for the opportunity, and Tom knew it. He was more than happy to wait; he certainly didn't want to pressure Tom out of his job. It was Charlie's dream and, since Tom had made the announcement that he was going to step down eventually and was looking for a worthy replacement, Charlie wanted to ensure he had the skills to make it work. He would be devastated if it all went wrong because he didn't know what he was doing.

Blowing out a breath fifteen minutes later, he had to admit defeat. He was the only bartender until six, but he was swamped.

"Bear with me, guys and gals," he called to the customers at the bar, "I'm calling reinforcements." Charlie grabbed the phone and dialled Analise's number. "Hey, Ana. Sorry to call, but is there any chance you can get here now? I don't know what's happened, but we're packed, and I'm barely keeping up." He was hot and sweaty, which was a terrible combination when working in a bar, but at least this bar had air conditioning.

"Of course, Charlie. I'll be there in ten." Analise rang off. Fortunately, she lived down the road, so Charlie knew ten minutes meant ten minutes.

Charlie turned. "Reinforcements will be here in ten!" A cheer went up from the customers, and Charlie got back to work. His mind went blank as he worked tirelessly, tending to customers as soon as he was able. He loved the customers. Most of them were regulars, like Johnson, and knew Charlie would get to them as soon as he could and were content to wait. Others grumbled but there was nothing he could do.

Analise came in ten minutes later, looking cool, calm and collected. She disappeared into the office, then ducked behind the bar counter to Charlie. Grabbing an apron, Analise pecked Charlie's cheek. "Hey, how's it rolling?"

Charlie loved Analise. She was the universal picture of perfection—blonde bombshell with long wavy hair, bright blue eyes, red pouty lips, toned legs and a nice rack. Charlie was gay but he could appreciate the beauty of the woman in front of him. No dumb blonde here, though—she was as sharp as a knife and never took crap from anyone. She was also the perfect friend a boy could have. They weren't like other friends; they weren't in each other's pockets all the time but still hung out and chatted often enough. More importantly, they were always there at the other end of the phone, dropping everything if the other needed anything.

"Good, thanks." Charlie swiped his forehead. "Thanks for coming in early. I've no idea what's got everyone here so early today." Charlie placed a row of shots in front of a boisterous group of girls, grabbed the money and turned to ring it up.

"Keep the change," came the slurred voice of one of the girls. Charlie half turned, making eye contact and thanked her. Collecting the change, he placed it in the tip jar, which was getting fuller by the minute.

"I heard on the grapevine Goode & Sons had won a huge contract and let everyone leave an hour earlier today. Don't know if it's true, but that could account for it," Analise commented as she started making orders. She lined up several glasses side by side, grabbed the vodka bottle and the coke spray and filled the glasses one by one never spilling a drop.

"Oh wow, that's good for them then. And, yes, it would explain all these happy people." Charlie chuckled.

He looked at the clock realising Tom would be in soon. As soon as he came in, Charlie could have his break. He'd been working since two and certainly needed it after this. The crowd was heaving, but everyone seemed in high spirits and were well mannered, so he couldn't ask for more.

Tom walked through the door, stopping with wide eyes, taking in all the customers. He side-stepped as a couple left, then headed over to the bar. "What in the name is going on?" he said, gazing around again.

Charlie laughed. "We got busy is what's going on. Just so you know, I called Analise in early!" Charlie switched places with Analise as they each needed different drinks. "Come on, boss, get your butt around here. I need a breather," Charlie blew out a breath, smirking as he caught a customer's eye roll. "What! You guys are wearing me out!"

The customer chuckled. "You don't seem like you're flagging." His gaze looked him up and down as far as he could from the other side of the bar, making Charlie's cheeks heat again. Charlie had not seen him before, but he was certainly worth looking at. "In fact, you seem positively on a roll. Why mess with perfection? I'm Max." Max kept his focus on Charlie as he reached his hand forward, shook Charlie's hand, then broke eye contact when Analise placed his drink in front of him. "Thanks." He winked at Charlie, then moved away.

"Phew, if looks could set you on fire…. Wow! Charlie, he's yours if you want him!" Analise fanned her face as she turned to him. "Look, Tom's here now. Why don't you have that break you're so desperately saying you need." She rested her hands on his shoulders and reached up on tiptoes, bringing her mouth near Charlie's ear, "You definitely need to cool down after that I think!" Analise smirked and batted his shoulder as she turned to speak to Tom.

Charlie flushed again and glanced back at the guy, catching him staring again. Blinking away quickly, he left the bar area, manoeuvring his way to the office and pushed through the door. He wouldn't say he was good looking himself—when he looked in the mirror, he saw an average looking, skinny, brown-haired guy with no distinguishable features—but he had been flirted with many times while he was working, though he didn't think anyone meant it as more than friendly banter.

As the door closed, it blocked some of the noise from the bar area. He stretched his arms above his head and yawned as he made his way to the fridge to grab his food. Working at the bar always gave him a high he couldn't get anywhere else, but he knew that if he sat down at that point, he would never get back up again.

Charlie heated his leftover lasagne in the microwave and emptied the salad onto the plate while he waited.

The microwave beeped so Charlie transferred the contents to his plate, taking it to the table while grabbing his phone along the way. Unlocking his phone, he saw he had three messages and a few emails. His stomach fluttered as he realised one of the messages was from Josh, so he kept that for last, eking out the anticipation. The other messages were from his mother, the first asking what time Charlie finished, and the second telling him to ignore the last message because she'd just asked Josh. Charlie shook his head and smiled. His mother was new to the mobile phone situation, so she was getting used to being in contact with Charlie all the time. Checking his emails and seeing they were not important, he turned to Josh's message.

He ran his finger over his name before opening it.

JOSH: *How you doing, pipsqueak?*

Charlie rested his head in his hand and laughed, the sound reverberating around the room. Pipsqueak! Josh was always coming up with different names for him but none of them stuck, thank god. At eighteen, Josh was a year younger than him, but he didn't act it. In fact, he acted older than Charlie. They attended the same parties mostly, had the same friends, even ran in the same social circles. The only difference was he worked at the bar and Josh was at college studying art. College was definitely not his thing, but he did enjoy the social aspects and was able to tag along with Josh if none of his own friends were going.

CHARLIE: *Lol, try again, buttbrain. Work is crazy busy. Apparently, Goode & Sons got a huge contract, so let everyone out early. I've been swamped since half four. What are you up to tonight? x*

Charlie typed the message as he ate his food, thinking back to that morning. He'd woken up early and walked into the bathroom with his eyes half shut. He'd sat on the toilet and before he had the chance to do anything, heard a groaning noise that hadn't come from him.

He snapped his eyes open, suddenly wide awake. Becoming more aware of his surroundings, he realised the shower was running. He zeroed in on the sight in front of him—Josh was standing under the spray, one hand resting on the wall, the other around his cock, moving it up and down the rock-hard shaft. When he heard a chuckle, his gaze flew up to Josh's eyes, seeing the grin on his face.

"Shit, sorry!" Charlie mumbled as he almost ran out of the bathroom, cheeks on fire. Closing the door behind him, he stood there, heart pounding, breath heaving, and leaned his head back against the door. He closed his eyes and muttered to himself, "Shit, shit, shit."

Closing his eyes was the worst idea though, as all he could see was Josh's more than impressive package. He inhaled and exhaled slowly, trying to calm his racing heart but sucked in another breath as he fell backwards when the door opened behind him.

Josh caught him around the waist, and Charlie grabbed for the door frame, making him stop quickly and smash his head into Josh's chin.

"Ouch!" Josh let him go once he was steady on his feet and rubbed his chin with a grimace. "No need to knock me out, the bathroom's all yours!" He moved out of the doorway, bowing and gesturing with his arm for him to enter. Josh continued to his bedroom, looking back at him before shutting his door. Charlie scrambled inside the bathroom and made sure to lock the door. God, what was wrong with him? First, he walked in on him, then he fell into his arms.

Coming back to the present, Charlie's breath was uneven, but this time he allowed his real feelings out. There was no one here to chastise him for his thoughts, only his own mind drudging up what society would say to him—*disgusting, vile, sickening, revolting*. His thoughts were not socially acceptable and never would be. They weren't to him either, but he couldn't stop himself.

He'd finally admitted a few weeks ago that he was physically attracted to Josh—to his brother. It had taken him by surprise the first time it happened. He had walked into the kitchen and had seen someone bending down by the dishwasher. Taking his time, appreciating how the ass looked in the tight jeans, he realised as he was about to say something crude, that it was Josh. He hadn't recognised him straight away because he had never seen Josh in tight jeans before—he always wore loose ones, so it had thrown him. Charlie had never been so glad to have stayed silent than he had at that moment.

Picturing Josh as he thrust his cock through his palm, even though it was only a glimpse, had him squirming on his chair, his own dick stiffened. He was a god to look at. Slightly taller than Charlie's five foot nine, Josh had the toned physique of the athlete that he was. He ran daily and everyone could tell. His hair was a gorgeous golden-brown colour, short on the sides and longer on top. Many a time since Charlie's revelation had he wanted to run his hands through it, but this new glimpse of Josh would fuel his dreams for months. It was all he could have. He was under no illusion they would live happily ever after, and he hoped, after allowing the thoughts to manifest, he would eventually find someone else to crush on.

He had to. There was no other option. Not for him.

2

Josh

J osh pulled his sweat-soaked top away from his chest as he walked up the front path. He'd pushed himself harder than ever, trying to run away from his demons. It hadn't worked.

He let himself into the house and ran upstairs without shouting out for anyone. He knew everyone was out or at work, so he had the place to himself. Shucking his top as he got to his room, he threw it towards the washing basket then removed the rest of his clothes. He grabbed his towel and marched, naked, towards the bathroom. Hopefully, the hot water would soothe his muscles, even if it couldn't settle his mind.

Aiden was driving him insane. His boyfriend thought it was okay to cancel dates left, right and centre with little or no notice. They were supposed to be checking out Trish's party tonight, but Aiden had called off saying he'd forgotten about dinner with his parents. Josh wasn't sure whether he believed him, but at least he had given him more than five minutes notice this time. He would usually ask Charlie, but he was at work, and he was more than happy to go stag anyway. Maybe he would nip into the bar on the way home to see his brother. He'd not seen him very much this week because Charlie was covering for staff holidays.

He chuckled. He hadn't been expecting to see him that morning because he knew Charlie had closed Crush the night before. He'd been in the middle of his routine morning jacking off session when the door had opened. Josh had watched as Charlie had stumbled his way to the toilet using his hands for guidance. He hadn't realised he was still stroking his cock until an unexpected surge of pleasure streamed through him as his brother dropped his pyjama bottoms. That was why he'd made a noise. He'd snorted when Charlie's eyes had snapped open and he'd almost run for the door.

Josh chuckled again as he turned on the shower. He doubted Charlie would do that again in a hurry. He washed himself clean with the usual soap, reminding himself about his agenda, feeling disappointed Aiden wouldn't be available for a little one on one action. With that thought, his cock began to harden. He smoothed one hand down his stomach and took hold of his dick tightly, the soap acting as a lubricant. Thinking about what he and Aiden had done last week, he slowly stroked himself until he hardened completely. Aiden was a gymnast; therefore, very flexible, which certainly made their sex life more adventurous. He was also feminine in his behaviour and speech, but masculine in his appearance—not Josh's usual type.

They had come home from a party and had gotten as far as Aiden's sofa before Josh had pressed him over the arm, head on the cushions. His ass was at the right height and in the perfect position for Josh. He stroked faster, remembering shoving down Aiden's trousers and seeing his top slide up his back.

"God, yes." He ran his palm over the head of his cock then tightened his grip further, stroking faster again. *Josh unfastened his own trousers, covered his cock in a condom, and after a few short moments of preparing him, sank into Aiden's ass in one go. "Fuck!" Josh held Aiden's hips as he impaled him over and over. Aiden clutched at the cushions, screaming Josh's name as he came. He rested his hand on Aiden's back, pushing up his top more to reveal his shoulders, then reaching around to pinch his nipples.*

Josh scrunched his forehead when a thought went through his head, but it flew out again the next minute when he began to come. As his release began in earnest, he imagined the guy below him taking his seed. "Fuck, yes, god, ah, fuck!" His release painted the shower walls as the guy lifted his head and smiled.

Josh rested his head against the wall. He was in so much trouble. "What the fuck?" he muttered as he got his breath back. It hadn't been Aiden he'd seen when the guy lifted his head. It had been Charlie.

· • • • ● • ◐ • • • ·

The "bathroom episode," as Josh had started calling it in his head, had left him off-kilter for the rest of the afternoon. He had tried painting to get his mind off it, but it kept popping up at any given moment. All he'd managed to do in the end was ruin two perfectly good canvasses, and he'd begun to get cranky. So, he'd given up on that and tried to finish an assignment that was due next week. That hadn't worked out either.

Therefore, he'd done the next best thing. He had called Chris, a fellow gym buddy who loved partying, and asked him if he could tag along with him to the party. Probably not his best idea because Chris would most likely be three sheets to the wind before an hour had passed, but it was a diversion, nonetheless. At least making sure Chris went home safely would give him something to think about, and with Aiden not being there, he could relax a little.

After about half an hour at the party, Kent called to him over the music then dropped himself on the seat next to Josh. "Hey, how're things?" He held a beer in one hand and with his other pulled Carla over to sit on his lap. Kent and Carla had been high school sweethearts and were still going strong. They had all been in the same year at school, and to his knowledge, neither eye ever strayed. They seemed built on strong foundations, especially as they had only been thirteen when they had started. He would happily admit he was jealous of them. Their relationship was the stuff of legends and fairy tales and it was what he wanted. He and Aiden were okay for now, but he knew they wouldn't be a forever thing.

"Alright, thanks. How are you?" Josh finished his beer and leaned forward to place it on the table.

"Good, good. Where's Aiden tonight?"

"He's—" Josh started.

"Kent, you just saw him with Seb, didn't you?" Carla was a happy, talkative drunk and was apparently well on her way there. She was also a very cute drunk. She held out her finger as if to touch Kent's nose but missed completely, nearly poking him in the eye instead. Kent grabbed her finger and kissed the tip.

"I didn't see him." Kent shrugged and turned to Josh. "I thought he'd be glued to your side. He normally is when you're together." He took a drink of his beer, looking at Josh.

"Carla must've been mistaken. Aiden had a family dinner tonight, so couldn't come." The feeling from earlier came back, and he wondered whether Aiden actually had a family dinner or if he was blowing him off. He went to get up when Carla stopped him with a hand on his arm.

"No, he's definitely here. I saw him going upstairs with Seb." Carla patted his cheek, then leaned back against Kent. Josh met Kent's eyes, knowing exactly what the other man was thinking because he was thinking it too.

Josh shook his head and got up. "Well I best be seeing what my guy is getting up to then, hadn't I?"

"Josh, I think we both know how this is going to end, don't we?" Kent said, holding his beer out as if to point. "I'm here if you need anything, man." Josh nodded, said goodbye to Carla then set off towards the staircase. Kent was right. He had a feeling he knew exactly where this night was headed, and it wasn't where he'd wanted it to go. But it also wasn't much of a surprise. He'd obviously subconsciously known this would happen because he wasn't as upset about it as he should have been. Maybe he should just leave instead.

He shook his head and stalked to the stairs, taking them two at a time. At the top, he asked someone if they had seen Aiden or Seb and they pointed to the bedroom on the far right of the hallway. Thanking them, knowing they wouldn't have been so forthcoming with directions had they known the potential result, he walked steadily to the door, took a deep breath and opened it. He saw Aiden, naked, ass in the air, deep throating Seb while Seb returned the favour. Just the visual he needed. At least he knew where they stood now.

He turned, walked down the stairs and grabbed Chris on his way as he stalked to the car, half carrying him—three sheets to the wind as predicted. After depositing Chris in the passenger seat, Josh jumped in and drove him home. Having seen Chris safely into his girlfriend's arms, he turned the car towards home. He definitely couldn't see Charlie now. Not with his mind in this condition. Okay, he wasn't upset the relationship was over, but he was pissed Aiden was cheating on him. How long had it been going on? How many other people knew he was being taken for a ride? One thing he was glad about now, was that he always wore condoms, even when Aiden said they didn't need to. It was one thing he'd never budged on.

Parking the car in the drive, he entered the house quietly as he knew Mum and Dad would be asleep by now. It was nearly ten but neither of them had ever been night owls. They'd be lucky to last until nine most nights. As teenagers who enjoyed going out, it was always a nightmare for him and Charlie. Their parents would stay up until they got home; therefore, knowing their parents were tired, they never stayed out late because they always felt bad about it. Not that their parents had ever complained about staying up to wait for them.

Josh climbed the stairs slowly, trying to avoid the creaky steps, and let himself into his room. Pushing the door closed, he ran his hand over his head and blew out a breath. Rubbing over his eyes to remove the scratchiness, he realised how tired he felt, and he hadn't done much all day. This situation with Aiden had taken something out of him. He stripped down to his boxers, threw his clothes in the basket, then laid back on the bed. He didn't know if he would sleep or not, but he got comfortable anyway.

3

Charlie

The following day, Charlie was able to rise at a reasonable time. Everyone had been asleep when he'd returned last night, and he hadn't wanted to make much noise, so took himself off to bed. It meant he'd had more than enough sleep, even though it was only eight-thirty. He had woken up several times though; dreams of him and Josh had been plentiful as usual. At least twice, he had woken on the cusp of orgasm and had finished himself off with his hand so he could go back to sleep.

But even with the broken sleep, he felt refreshed. He put some pyjama trousers on and meandered downstairs to the sound of conversation and the smell of pancakes. Pancakes meant one thing in this house: Josh was home.

Charlie felt his heart skip a beat and told himself to stop. At least this time when he saw Josh, he'd be wearing something a little less revealing. He walked into the kitchen, kissing his dad's cheek as he passed him as his dad left the room. Rounding the corner, he froze briefly, seeing Josh sat at the table in joggers. It wasn't very often he saw him lounging without a top on, but it was a beautiful sight when he did. Josh didn't have a lot of muscle definition, but Charlie knew he ran and did some weights, and it certainly showed in his arms. He ignored the thrum in his lower stomach and carried on to the table, snagging a piece of bacon from the pan along the way.

"Good morning, sunshine," Mum said, reaching up to kiss Charlie's cheek. "You're up earlier than I expected."

"Morning. Yeah, I was home by eleven-thirty last night, so went straight to bed. I've had plenty of sleep, so thought I'd join you for breakfast for a change." Charlie sat on a chair next to Josh, folding a leg underneath him.

Josh smirked. "We are truly honoured by your presence," he said, inclining his head.

Charlie hid a smile and threw a bit of pancake at him. "Shut up."

"Now, now, children. Let's be adults, please," Mum called from behind them.

Charlie stuck his tongue out at Josh, frowning slightly as Josh just stared at him without responding. Josh seemed to jerk himself out of his stupor and grinned.

"So, what are you working today? It's your closing day, isn't it?" Josh inquired, raising his eyebrows and grabbing some more pancakes.

He hesitated. "I was supposed to, but I've got a date, so I'm working two to ten today." Charlie hadn't wanted to mention the date, but he wasn't sure how else he could explain why he wasn't there if Josh came into the bar to see him. He thought being honest would save any further questions.

"Ooh, who's the lucky guy?" his mum asked, coming to sit at the table with yet another plate of pancakes. His mum looked good for her fifty-nine years of age. She had started to go a little grey, but her deep laughter lines showed she had lots of joy in her life. She always said that she didn't mind growing old because it just meant it was another year she got to spend with them. Charlie had always loved that saying, and it was one he hoped he would live by when he got older. His mother was shorter than him but had such a big personality that it rarely showed.

"No one you know, just a guy I met at the bar." He didn't lie exactly. There was that guy, Max, at the bar who had asked him out last night, but that wasn't who he was seeing.

"Where are you going? Don't you think you should find out more about him before being alone with him?" The barked questions had come from Josh, and Charlie looked over in surprise. Josh's eyes were narrowed, and a pulse twitched at his temple. The whiteness around his lips advertised his anger.

Charlie lifted his chin. "And how exactly am I supposed to get to know him without going out on a date with him, huh?" He pinned Josh with his gaze in defiance, then frowned and shook his head.

"Well, going on a date sounds nice to me. At least you are getting yourself out there instead of staying behind that bar. You need more socialising than those parties the two of you keep going to." Mum put two pancakes on her plate and covered them with a small amount of syrup.

Changing the subject, Charlie asked, "Are you off to college today, J?"

Josh inhaled, and his forehead cleared. "Yeah, my first class is at ten, then I finish at one. I'm going to head to the studio for a couple of hours after." From under his eyelashes, Charlie watched him mop up the last of the syrup with the pancakes, shove it in his mouth then rub his hands together. Picking up his plates, Josh opened the dishwasher and placed them in gently and shut the door again. Charlie watched the play of muscles along his back, remembering the other time he'd seen Josh do the same thing. Rounding the table to Mum, Josh pecked her on the cheek and said, "See you later, I'm off for a run."

"Bye sweetheart, have fun."

"See ya." Charlie looked down at his plate, moving the food from side to side. *Why was Josh going for a run just after eating?* Brushing it off, he considered his plans. In some ways, he couldn't wait for the date tonight, but in others, he could. It wasn't his best option, only a much-needed one. Jimmy would do what he asked of him, mainly because it was what he wanted anyway. They both knew what they would get out of it. That's why he'd chosen him.

• • • ● ● • ● ● • • •

"Right, I'm off to work!" Charlie called several hours later, running down the stairs, swinging his coat behind him.

"Charlie!" Josh shouted after him, startling Charlie to a stop on the bottom step.

"Shit, Josh, you made me jump. I thought you were still out."

"Nah, I couldn't be bothered to stay after all. Do me a favour. If Aiden turns up, refuse to sell him alcohol for me," he said, slowly descending the stairs. He noticed Josh wasn't smiling like he usually did when he was joking.

Charlie narrowed his eyes. "What's the asshole done?"

"It's *who* he hasn't done that's the issue," he said, rolling his eyes. "Apparently, he's a *very* popular student. Just not for the reasons I thought." Josh walked past him and into the hallway, shoulders slumped.

"Shit, J. Well, he's definitely not worth it. Chin up, bro, there's plenty of guys out there for you. Just be patient." Charlie's heart broke for him. Yes, he knew Aiden was an ass and had warned Josh previously, but he also knew Josh had to find out for himself. He hated that he was right, though.

Looking at Charlie, Josh murmured, "Yeah, I know." He shook his head slowly. "I'm more annoyed because I didn't know about it. I can't believe I didn't realise what was going on," he said, leaning against the wall and crossing his arms over his chest. Charlie walked over to him, standing in front of him.

Reaching his hand up to cup Josh's chin, he said, "You'll be fine. Be patient, give it time. You're only eighteen." Charlie rubbed along his cheek, feeling the scratch of the stubble. He caught himself before he shivered. "I've got to go. See you later, baby brother!" Charlie reached up onto his toes to press a kiss to Josh's cheek, then waved before scampering out the house.

"I'm one year younger than you, Charlie! One year!" Josh grumbled after him.

• • • ● ●•● ● •• •

"What can I get you?" Charlie wiped the counter in front of the customer who had just arrived.

"Bourbon on the rocks, please. And keep them coming." His voice was soft and not quite in tune with his wrinkled suit. He looked like he'd had a hard day and his words proved it. Charlie watched him from the corner of his eye as he went about preparing the drink order. The guy blew out a breath as he settled on the stool, linking his fingers together in front of him and looking down at them. He was gorgeous, even in his melancholy.

"I have an ear should you need it," Charlie said quietly, placing the drink in front of him.

"Huh?" he said, looking up at him as if he wasn't expecting Charlie to be there. He seemed to realise where he was and what Charlie had said at the same time. "Uh, thanks. I'll keep that in mind." He picked up the drink, studied it briefly and downed it in one go, pushing the glass back to him once it was empty.

"No problem." Charlie went about making another drink for him, noticing another customer at the other end of the bar needed service. He placed the drink in front of the guy. "You know where to find me. Just shout for Charlie," he said to him, tapping the bar before moving to the other customer.

Charlie looked at his watch. One hour left before his shift was over. He had a date to get ready for. Okay, maybe it wasn't so much of a date as a hookup, but he had chosen Jimmy because he knew he'd get the job done. He also knew Jimmy was not the best choice, but he didn't have many people to choose from. He was nineteen for Christ's sake; he needed to get laid.

He spent the hour filling drink orders, cleaning behind the bar and keeping an eye on that customer who still looked so weary. Although he had told Charlie to keep the drinks coming, the guy had only requested two more drinks and each one was finished slower than the last. Charlie wasn't worried about him now, only a little sad for him. He had seen many a person come in looking like him and go out incoherent. Those he worried about. This customer seemed to have some sense. He made a mental note to mention it to Analise when she took over though, just to be sure.

He finished putting the last glasses in the dishwasher and set it going.

"Hey, Charlie. How's it hanging?" Analise arrived while he was chopping some more lemon slices.

"Hey. Yeah good. Thanks for covering for me today." Charlie finished and put them in a dish, then washed his hands. He was glad to be finishing but not so enthused about his next visit. He supposed that should tell him something. He looked over to his customer. "Keep an eye on that guy for me."

"Why? Is he going to be an issue?" Analise eyed him critically.

Charlie looked over at him, seeing he was more relaxed than when he entered but looking into his glass as if it held the answers to the world. "No, I don't think so. He's on his fourth bourbon, but he's had it for a while now. I think he's finished, but just in case. Hang on." He touched Analise's shoulder and walked over to the customer. "Hey, are you doing okay?"

The customer looked up at him and gave a small smile. "Yeah, I'm good, thanks. Had a rough day."

"We all get them. Well, I'm heading off, so I'll leave you with Analise now." Charlie indicated over his shoulder to her.

"Thanks, Charlie. I appreciate it." He smiled again, and Charlie realised it didn't quite reach his eyes. "Oh, and I'm Sean."

"Nice to meet you. Enjoy your drink." Charlie walked back over to Analise. "Nah, he'll be no issue at all. I doubt he will even order another drink, to be honest. Anyway, thanks again for this. I'll see you tomorrow."

"See ya later, Charlie. Have a good one." Analise put her finger up to a customer telling them she'd be a minute then tied an apron around her waist. Charlie walked through the bar towards the office to collect his coat and nipped to the bathroom to freshen up his hair. Looking at his reflection, he ran his hands along his head, smoothing strands down as he went. He debated whether to style it more, but he knew his hair wouldn't stay in this weather. He left it as it was, knowing Jimmy wouldn't care, either way.

Charlie second-guessed himself again—or was it third- or fourth- guessed? What was he doing? He didn't care that every other man—and woman—he knew had jumped on the Jimmy bandwagon. That was the reason he'd made this decision. He knew Jimmy had no morals about fucking anyone. And he needed a result fast.

He splashed cold water on his face then gathered his coat and exited the bar. Crush was located in a nice part of town, which was another reason why he liked it so much. In a couple of years, the bar would hopefully be his to manage. That is unless Tom left before then, but he didn't see it happening. Crush was in Tom's blood as much as Charlie's if not more.

He walked down the street towards Mikey's where he was meeting Jimmy. That was not a bar he would usually frequent, but it was a means to an end. He walked through the door, feeling his shoes stick to the floor. Wincing, he carried on towards the bar where he'd seen Jimmy.

Jimmy was good looking and he knew it. He had short blond hair, chiselled jaw and was athletically built. If Charlie hadn't gone to school with him, he would have approached him had he seen him socially. Unfortunately, he knew exactly what he was like and he was an ass, not to put too fine a point on it.

"Hey, doll," Jimmy drawled, swinging around in his seat. "You ready for me?" Did he mention he was sleazy? And an ass.

"Hey, Jimmy. Sure, let's go." Charlie turned around and exited the bar, waiting for Jimmy on the path. He felt his arm go around his shoulders and tried not to flinch, although he couldn't stop himself from gritting his teeth.

"Okay, doll, let's head around the back." Jimmy steered him towards the back of the bar. Once they rounded the corner, Charlie dropped his coat and let out a hard breath when his back hit the wall. Jimmy's body slammed against his front, and he grabbed Charlie's face, trying to plant his lips against him.

Charlie struggled to turn his head away from the onslaught. "Jimmy, stop." He pushed at his chest.

"Why? You want me to fuck you, so here we are." Jimmy's hands reached down to Charlie's backside, gave it a squeeze then slid around the front to his button. Before Charlie knew it, Jimmy had the button undone and was pushing his hand down the front of his trousers, using his weight to keep Charlie flat against the wall. Jimmy had several pounds on Charlie, making it difficult to move.

Charlie frantically got his hands in between them and tried to push him away. "Wait!" He managed to move away from him slightly. "Not here."

Jimmy moved back towards him. "You wanted a fuck. I have things to do. I don't have time to be lovey-dovey about this. Come on. You know this is what you were after." He reached towards Charlie's open trousers again.

"No, Jimmy, we're not doing it." He pushed Jimmy away from him harder and rebuttoned his trousers, sighing out a deep breath. "Forget it, Jimmy, this was a bad idea." He tried to collect his thoughts, then reached down for his coat. As he bent, Jimmy pressed up against his ass, digging his erection into him. Charlie yelped, not having expected it, and nearly fell forward onto the ground. It was only Jimmy's hands steadying him that stopped his momentum, but Jimmy ground Charlie back against him.

"We're not done, Charlie. You asked for this, so I'm giving it to you." He ran one hand up under his top towards his shoulders and the other went to his front again, going for his button.

Charlie pushed his backside against Jimmy firmly, causing him to groan, then scrambled forward, escaping from his roaming hands. "I said forget it! I'm not doing this with you. Go back to your friends." He collected his things, this time making sure he kept Jimmy in sight.

"Fuck you, Charlie. You think you're all high and mighty, but you still come to me when you need something. No more favours for you. Stupid bitch!" Jimmy shouted as he stormed back towards the bar.

Great, no doubt his reputation will be ruined by morning. Jimmy wouldn't tell people Charlie refused. Oh no, he will most likely start a rumour about how Charlie sleeps with everyone and everything and maybe throw in some bondage along the way.

"Fuck." He blew out a breath, rubbing his hands over his face, now he knew Jimmy was gone. He gathered his coat and began the walk home; slower than usual. He didn't want to get there any time soon. He needed a shower when he got home. That thought made him walk quicker, even with so many other thoughts running around his head. It was beginning to get unbearable being around Josh. He needed his virginity out of the way, and maybe he'd stop having these thoughts about his brother. That sounded bad. Charlie closed his eyes, breathing deeply. He allowed his favourite image to run through his head for a moment, then cut it off, muttering, "Stop it, Charlie. Just stop it!"

• • • ● ● • ● ● • • •

Reaching home, Charlie went straight to his room. His parents were on an unusual night out with their friends, and Josh had a party, so he was all by himself. He could wallow in misery all alone—after a shower.

"For God's sake!" Charlie cursed, throwing his coat on the bed. He stood there, hands on hips, shaking his head. He should have known better. Jimmy was a selfish asshole, but he hadn't realised how much until an hour ago.

"Charlie?" Josh came through his door with a concerned look on his face. His younger brother was his best friend; they were closer to each other than anyone else. "What's wrong?"

Charlie jumped, having not expected him to be there. He was about to ask why he wasn't at the party, but his mouth dried up, and he just looked at him for a moment. Josh's hair was wet; he'd obviously just had a shower, although he was clothed. Shame. He shifted his thoughts again. If he told Josh what had happened, he wouldn't be surprised about Jimmy's behaviour, but he would be about Charlie and Jimmy. He sighed. Charlie needed to tell him; he never kept anything from him. Well...almost anything.

"Jimmy." He gave him a pointed look.

Josh raised his eyebrows, eyes wide.

"I know, I know. I shouldn't have trusted him. I just thought I'd finally get kissed!" His eyes went wide then he covered his face with his hands and threw himself on the bed, face first. "Shit, Shit, Shit!" His words were muffled in the covers.

"Charlie?"

He scrambled upright. "Never mind! I need a shower!" He tried to stand up, but Josh caught his arm, pulling him back.

"Woah, woah, woah! Hold on." Josh wrapped an arm around his waist, walked backwards a step and sat on the bed with Charlie almost sat on his knee. "Wait a minute. What do you mean *finally get kissed?*"

Charlie continued to struggle against his hold. "Nothing! Let me go!"

"CHARLIE!" Josh shouted his name.

He stopped struggling and closed his eyes in defeat. Josh gentled his hold, moving him to sit next to him on the bed but keeping his arm around him. "What are you talking about?" he asked softly.

Charlie sighed and relaxed into him. "I've never been kissed, so I..." he said quietly, looking at the floor. Josh didn't say anything for a minute, making him tense again. "Never mind. Forget I said anything!"

"Shh, it's okay." Josh rubbed his hand along Charlie's arm. "It's okay."

They sat quietly for a moment, then Charlie tucked his head between Josh's neck and shoulder, tears of mortification slowly dripping down to wet his brother's shirt. He could feel Josh's heartbeat increasing, and Charlie wanted to calm him. At the same time, he cursed himself for allowing himself to be so close to Josh when he had told himself not to get into this situation.

"Did he hurt you?" Josh's voice rumbled through his chest, the growl barely concealing his anger.

"No. He wanted a quickie up against the wall behind the bar before his friends turned up," he said, wincing as Josh cursed. Quickly, he carried on, "I told him where to go and left. Nothing else happened." He wasn't going to explain fully.

Josh took a couple of deep breaths, and Charlie felt him relaxing. Josh's hand came up to brush against his hair in soothing motions. After a few minutes, Josh pulled back, cupping his cheek to wipe away the last tears. He looked all over his face. "Why didn't you tell me?"

"I knew you'd be angry at me for going on a date with him—" he said quickly.

"No, not about Jimmy," Josh interrupted, shaking his head, then he frowned. "Although, we *will* talk about that later."

Charlie could feel his heart rate increasing. Josh was looking at him with a question in his eyes, and a little hurt too. He put his hand on Josh's chest, trying to soothe him, but also gently pushing him away. He was much too close to him, especially as he had kept another secret from him, that he didn't want his body to reveal. Josh wouldn't let him move back, he kept his arm around his waist and his hand cupping his cheek, eyes roaming across his face.

Charlie needed to get away from him. He moved his head away from his hand. "Let me go," he whispered.

"Wait," Josh said, voice rough. He stopped, looking at him, an indecipherable expression on his face. He licked his lips. "Can I..."

Charlie noticed Josh's breath puffing out fast onto his face. With any other person, he would assume they wanted him. He knew he felt something for Josh that was not socially acceptable, but that was his secret to bear; he couldn't go projecting his feelings. Josh licked his lips again, moving his hand to brush his thumb under his bottom lip. Charlie blinked, breath catching in his throat, eyes wide.

Josh froze and whispered, "Can I kiss you?" Charlie saw the panic, shame and heat flare in his brother's eyes.

He couldn't allow Josh to cross that line out of sympathy, so shook his head. "We can't," he returned quietly, his gaze caught on Josh's eyes. "You're my brother."

"I know. But..." Josh appeared caught up in the moment, un-caring of the consequences of this decision. Charlie knew what would happen after—Josh would feel disgusted, and they'd lose the relationship they had now.

However, Charlie hesitated, if Josh persisted, he knew he'd not have enough strength to pull away. In his dreams, he'd allowed this to happen and had been mortified when he'd woken. It had not stopped him from admiring and dreaming about Josh in secret.

"*Please*," Josh begged.

Charlie lost the battle. He nodded, fear and recklessness fluttering in his stomach.

Charlie groaned as Josh closed the gap between their lips. The first brush was just that—a small motion against his bottom lip. He released his breath against Josh's mouth in one big puff and he could hear the shakiness of it. He could also hear the panting noise he'd started making. What was he doing? But he couldn't fight it. Pleasure started to fork down his body to his cock. He had made himself come many times in the past, but nothing could have prepared him for the feeling invoked from someone else touching him, even this tiny amount.

Charlie closed the gap this time; his instincts made him shakily peck Josh's lips with gentle kisses. At this moment, he didn't care that he had no experience, he wanted Josh closer. His hands slid up Josh's chest, one going around his neck, the other into his hair. Josh groaned again, pressing their mouths harder. He felt Josh's tongue sliding along his lips, asking for entry. He never imagined how erotic that would feel and enjoyed the feel of it for a moment, then let his head drop back as he gave permission. The taste of Josh burst into his mouth as he explored the new area.

Charlie clutched at him, trying to get closer. Josh grabbed him by the waist and lifted him to straddle his legs. Arms closed around his back and fingers into his hair while Josh never once stopped the kiss. He felt himself squirming against Josh, reaching even closer. Josh moved a hand to his ass, pulling against Charlie to move him closer. The moment he did, he felt Josh hard against him. Charlie gasped, unable to stop himself from moving against him. Even though he knew it was wrong, he couldn't get enough. Even though he was running out of breath, he couldn't bring himself to stop.

Josh must have realised though because he broke the kiss, moving his mouth down Charlie's neck, painting it with his tongue and lips. Charlie gasped for breath as he continued to rock his body and cling to Josh's hair. He could feel his orgasm coming and had a moment of panic this was happening with his brother. His rhythm stuttered slightly, but then Josh kissed his mouth again and it was gone, replaced by bliss. Josh placed both hands on Charlie's hips and guided his motions on him. Josh hit the spot every time, and Charlie was nearly there.

"Oh, God! Fuck, I'm gonna come!" Charlie cried as he tore his mouth away. Josh mouthed at the base of his throat, just above his t-shirt. His breath hot and wet against Charlie, Josh slid one hand to the front and palmed his pecs, grazing his nipple with his nail. "Fu-uck!" Charlie arched his back, grabbing Josh's head to his chest as he came, waves crashing over him again and again. Josh kept the motion going, breathing harder and licked what skin he could reach.

"Shit, Charlie! Fuck!" Josh pressed tightly against him, wrapping his arms around his back and rested his face in Charlie's neck.

They stayed like that for a while, each breathing onto the skin of the other while their heartbeats returned to normal. Charlie was the first to move, bringing his head back to look at Josh, hands still around Josh's neck. He looked Josh in the eyes, trying to see if he regretted what happened.

Charlie released a breath, then realised he'd dry-humped Josh and hadn't done anything for him. His face burned with embarrassment as he cried, "Oh, God, I'm so sorry, I didn't think about you! I'm so embarrassed, rocking against you like that. Do you, um, need some help?" He blushed even brighter red, and Josh laughed a little.

"Nah, I'm all good," Josh said, going a little pink himself. "You already helped." He looked down into his lap and Charlie followed his gaze, noticing a wet patch on the front of his trousers. Josh gave him a quirky smile, then rubbed his hands up and down Charlie's back. He could see the knowledge in Josh's eyes before he spoke; his eyes turned sad.

"We can't do that again," Charlie whispered.

"I know," Josh said, resting their foreheads together.

"Thank you, Josh. I know it went further than you wanted, but my first kiss will definitely be remembered," Charlie said, stroking his cheek.

"Charlie, look at me." Josh used his hand to keep Charlie's chin up so he could see his eyes. "As much as it would be better for me to deny this, I wanted this. Wanted you. I don't know why I feel this way but never think I didn't want to do this with you." Josh kissed him. "You're amazing, and at this moment, I wish we weren't brothers. Thank you for allowing me this." He brushed his hand down Charlie's cheek and kissed him briefly again. "But now, I need to go; otherwise, I won't stop myself from going further. And I have to." He kissed him one final time and gently lifted him from his lap, sitting Charlie on the bed.

Josh stood up from the bed with a slight grimace and walked to the door. He hesitated at the doorway, looking back at Charlie with a sad smile. Then he turned and left.

Charlie stayed on his bed, tears running down his face. He covered his mouth, trying to muffle the sobbing. He laid on the bed, smothering his face in the covers. What had he done? How were they going to look at each other ever again? Why was he so sad when he thought about this never happening again? So many questions, so few answers.

4

Josh

"**S**hit, shit, shit! You stupid asshole!" Josh grabbed his head in his hands as he walked into his bedroom, kicking the door closed. "What the fuck have you done!"

He dropped onto his bed, resting his elbows on his knees, hands still on his head. He couldn't believe he'd done that to Charlie. Fuck, it had been better than he'd imagined the couple of times his brain had overridden his dreams, but damn, it *shouldn't* have happened. What was Charlie going to think of him? He wouldn't be able to look Charlie in the eye ever again, but every time Josh caught a glimpse of him, he would remember. And now, they would have to hide their transgression from everyone they knew.

He rubbed his face with his hands before pushing them through his hair again and resting them, linked, on the back of his neck.

"Anyone home?" Dad shouted from downstairs. "I have Chinese, and I'm willing to eat it all myself!" Josh heard his dad laugh followed by banging in the kitchen beneath his room.

"This is going to be fun," he muttered as he got up. "Yeah, Dad, I'm here. Make sure you leave some for me." Josh tried to put some pep in his voice. He quickly changed his clothes, cleaning off his come. He opened his door, looking at Charlie's as he walked past,

30

wondering whether he would come down or stay in his room. He wasn't sure which he wanted him to do, to be honest.

Descending the stairs, running his hand along the bannister as if he could delay the inevitable, he took a deep breath when he got to the bottom and put more of a spring in his step as he entered the kitchen. "Hey. What's this in aid of?" His eyes went wide at the amount of food that was being removed from the bags. "How many people are you feeding?"

"Ha ha, very funny. I know how fussy you are, so I brought several different items. There should be at least one thing you like."

"Where's Mum? I thought you went out with your friends?" Josh asked while he searched for plates.

"Um, she stayed out with a friend." Josh turned to ask more when he saw his dad's eyes light up. "Hey Charlie, what are you doing here? I wasn't expecting you until late. I was going to keep you some to heat up when you'd finished your shift." Dad pulled Charlie to him and kissed his cheek. Charlie looked a little pale, but there were no signs of any upset.

"Thanks, Dad. I got Analise to cover half of my shift. Felt like having a breather." Charlie didn't look at Josh, just moved around their dad to reach for the cutlery. Bringing them to the table, he reached for the sweet and sour chicken at the same time as Josh did. "Oh, sorry, you have it."

"Nah, it's okay, you first." Josh removed his hand and pulled out a chair to sit down.

Dad raised his eyebrows. "Okay, who are you and what have you done with my son?" he asked, staring at Josh.

Josh's cheeks heated, and he stared at the table. "Shut up," he said without force.

"And you're back." His dad laughed. "Never mind, I don't want to know. I'm going to take a quiet, calm evening instead of the usual boisterous one if you're giving me it!" Dad picked his food choices and filled his plate. "I'm even going to sit in the lounge and watch TV while I eat. If anyone wants to join me, you know where I'll be." Dad headed out of the kitchen.

Josh and Charlie were quiet while they filled their plates. If they reached for the same thing, they both jerked their hands back quickly. Finally, Josh had had enough.

"Charlie, we have to try and get back to normal," he pleaded, his voice low. "Dad has already noticed something isn't right, and we've only been with him ten minutes. I'm sorry I've put you in this position. I should have had more restraint. I'm sorry." Josh filled his plate and started to leave. "I'll eat upstairs out of your way."

"Wait, Josh." He stopped near the door with his back to the kitchen. "Come back to the table," Charlie said quietly. Josh looked at him over his shoulder, his eyes sad but welcoming. He hesitated, and Charlie held out his palm, wiggling his fingers at him. "Sit with me. Eat." Josh took his place at the table next to him, trying to ignore how close they were. He needed to figure out how to push everything he was feeling back inside him so it wouldn't show, like before. But after tasting him, holding him, feeling him come, he didn't know if he could do it.

At first, there was silence, except for the sounds of chewing and swallowing—neither of them trying to catch the other's eye.

"It's not your fault, Josh." Charlie's quiet voice interrupted the silence.

Josh looked to the doorway, listening for their dad, then returned his gaze to him. "Yes, it is. If I hadn't asked if I could kiss you, we wouldn't be in this situation now." He shook his head, moving his food around on his plate before starting to bite his fingernails. He jumped when he felt Charlie's hand on his, pulling it away from his mouth.

"Stop that. You only do it when you're worried." He squeezed his hand gently after resting it on the table between them. "Okay,

I'll change my wording slightly. It's not *just* your fault. I had every chance to stop it and I didn't. We need to figure out a way to put it behind us. To get back to where we were." Charlie stared at their hands as he talked. He took a deep breath and released it shakily. "I will say though…" He glanced up at Josh from under his eyelashes, smiling and whispered so quietly, "My first kiss was amazing."

Josh blushed hard but didn't look away. Their breathing seemed loud in the quiet kitchen. They both jumped apart when their dad entered the kitchen, neither of them had heard him coming. Josh stared at his plate, allowing a small smile to stay on his face while he finished his food. Idle chatter resumed around him, and he heard his dad ask Charlie a question. As the voices rumbled around him, his mind wandered back to what happened, and he still couldn't believe it had.

"…don't you think? Josh?" his dad's question shattered his thoughts and pulled him back to the present.

"Sorry, what?" Josh blinked up at him.

"I was saying maybe Charlie could teach you some bar work for when you go to uni? You may need, or want, to get a part-time job. I'm sure there will be plenty of bars around the place. What do you think?"

Several things went through Josh's mind at that moment in time. Firstly, nothing at all healthy—something to do with leaning Charlie over the bar when it was closed. Secondly, how difficult it would be to see and talk to him in close quarters for any length of time though unable to touch him. And finally, how could get out of this to stop any of the previous thoughts from becoming reality.

"Err…I don't know if I'd be any good at that…it's Charlie's thing, not mine." He tried to put Dad off, but apparently, he was having none of it.

"Just give it a try, eh? Charlie, you're working Sunday, aren't you? Why don't you take him with you for a couple of hours? See what happens. If he's rubbish, you can tell him so!" Dad laughed, unaware of the uncomfortable looks Josh and Charlie swapped. His dad squeezed his shoulder as he walked back to the lounge.

"Fuck," Josh said as he closed his eyes, leaned forward and rested his forehead on the table.

"Fuck," Charlie repeated. At least they had three days to get used to the idea.

• • • ● ●•● ● •• •

Josh spent the following day at college, attending classes and doing his homework in the library. He avoided going home when he knew he might see Charlie. Cowardly? Maybe. Self-preserving? Definitely. He didn't know what his reaction would be when he saw him so tried to avoid him. He understood he'd be working at the bar with him—thanks to Dad—but it was two days away. It didn't mean he had to deal with it now.

What the hell had he been thinking? Charlie probably hated him now even if he seemed okay about it all. Josh shook his head, trying to get back to his work. He'd read the same paragraph fifty times already but knew he had to do something to try and get his mind off the situation. He started again, scribbling down notes ready to write the assignment later.

Finally, he looked at his watch and realised he couldn't wait any longer. He needed to head home because he'd told his mother he would help her with dinner. Pulling all his things together, he shoved them into his bag and threw it over his shoulder. Picking up his phone, he saw a message from Kent.

KENT: *Party tonight at mine, be there for 8.*

A party at Kent's might be just what he needed. There would be several guys in need of a good time. He needed a night out.

JOSH: *I'll be there.*

He replied to Kent while walking out of the library, not looking where he was going. He bumped into someone and dropped his phone. Luckily, it didn't smash.

"I'm sorry, I didn't see—" He started to apologise as he picked up his phone, then looked up and saw Aiden standing there with a smile on his face. "What do you want?" he snapped.

"Is that any way to talk to your boyfriend?" Aiden tried to drape himself against Josh's side like he used to, but Josh pushed him away. His smile fell. "What the hell? Why are you being like this? I thought you'd be eager as we've not seen each other for two days." He stood there and crossed his arms, a pout on his lips.

"I've not seen you for two days because I didn't want to." Josh strode away, down the steps of the library towards the car park, where he'd left the car.

"Sweetheart, what's the matter?" Josh listened as Aiden tried to keep up with him, but he didn't slow his speed like he usually would. "Slow down, honey, I can't keep up."

He kept going, heading for his car and reaching for the keys in his pocket. Aiden grabbed his arm, making his keys fall out of his hand to the ground. "What is the matter with you?" he shouted as he pushed Aiden's arm off his and snatched up his keys. He carried on towards his car, getting more annoyed as time went on.

"Josh! What has gotten into you?" Aiden shrieked behind him.

Josh rounded on him. "Me? What has gotten into *me*? Maybe I should be asking what's gotten into you? Or rather *who*?" Josh could see some students looking over at them, so he tried to leave again, but Aiden was having none of it.

"What are you talking about?" he asked with a frown.

He rounded on him again. "Did you have fun with Seb?" Josh cocked his head, staring at him full on, watching as understanding dawned in his eyes.

Aiden was flustered. "I don't know what you mean. What are you accusing me of?" he said quietly, darting his eyes around them as he moved nearer.

"I'm not *accusing* you of anything. I saw it with my own eyes. And I really don't care anymore. You're welcome to him and any of the others you have slept with. Have fun!" He smirked, finger waved then turned and finished the distance to his car. Josh shoved his bag on the car seat, quickly got in and slammed the door when he heard Aiden calling him again. He took a deep breath, started the engine and drove home, shaking his head. He hoped it would be the last he'd have to deal with him, but he had a feeling it wouldn't be as easy as that. Aiden was very high maintenance.

His mind wandered to Aiden's potential indiscretions the whole journey home. Parking up, he grabbed his things and went in the door, shouting hello as he went. Putting his bag at the bottom of the stairs ready to take up later, he pocketed his keys while he walked towards the kitchen. He could hear his mum laughing and smiled. His mum was awesome. She was ready for anything at any time and it always seemed to be what he or Charlie needed at that moment.

He rounded the corner and hesitated when he saw Charlie standing with their mother at the counter.

"Josh! Did you have a good day at college?" His mum turned her cheek up to him, and he approached for a kiss.

"Yes, thanks. Managed to get some work done at the library." He paused before going over to Charlie and kissing his cheek too.

Mum would probably notice if he didn't as it had always been something he'd done. He was second-guessing every move he made around him, now.

Charlie smiled as he accepted the token, but still blushed a little. It made Josh's heart clench and his cock strain. Seeing him all rosy reminded him of times that needed to be forgotten. He turned away, trying to adjust himself discreetly.

"What do you need me to do, Mum?" he asked, going to the sink to wash his hands.

"If you can prepare the veg that's on the table, please, Josh." His mum was standing at the second sink, peeling potatoes and passing them over to Charlie for him to cut and place in the pan.

"What are we having?" Josh went around the table, sat and started in on the carrots.

"Shepherd's pie." Josh's stomach decided to rumble at that moment, making everyone laugh. "Soon, Rumbly Bear, soon," chuckled his mother, using the nickname from when he was younger. She had always told him she had never been able to feed him enough; therefore, his tummy was always rumbling.

$$\bullet \; \bullet \; \bullet \; \bullet \; \bullet \bullet \; \bullet \; \bullet \; \bullet \; \bullet \; \bullet$$

Dinner had been a quiet affair, and Charlie had rushed off after to start his shift. Josh had helped do the dishes, and then went upstairs to get ready for the party. Throwing his bag on the bed, he stripped down for a shower. Remembering what happened the last time his thoughts wandered, he avoided starting something in there and quickly washed and dried. Opening his wardrobe, he rummaged through to find a shirt and some jeans from the dresser. He was going to make an effort tonight.

Getting dressed, he checked the clock realising he was going to be late, and he hurried through his routine. Although Kent probably wouldn't care, he hated letting people down. Rushing down the stairs, he shouted goodbye to his parents and drove to Kent's house. He'd decided to drive so he wouldn't make a fool out of himself and so he could offer a ride to a beautiful guy should he wish to.

Parking wasn't too bad; it would get worse as the night progressed. Locking the car and pocketing his keys, he walked up the drive and into the house. Music pumped from the stereo, and he saw several people he knew straight away, nodding to them as he passed, searching for Kent. He found him holding vigil in the kitchen, arm around Carla as usual and laughing his ass off.

"What's so funny?" Josh asked, smiling.

Kent had to compose himself before he looked up at Josh, grimacing. "Tate was telling me he was in the car park when you had the tiff with Aiden this afternoon. I'm not laughing at you, J. He was saying how pissed Aiden looked after you screeched away in the car. Sorry, man." Kent did look ashamed, but Josh understood.

"Nah, don't worry. I gave him a mouthful, all right. I doubt he'll come back anymore. Which I'm more than happy about now." Josh reached across the counter to grab a beer, more than ready for one, even if it could only be one. He was second-guessing his stance on driving here now. He may have to grab a taxi home after all. "Won't be easy avoiding him since we're in the same social circles." He took a deep drink.

"I wouldn't worry about it. Start flirting with a few guys, he'll soon get the picture," laughed Tate, high-fiving his neighbour.

"So, Kent, what's the occasion for this get-together? It's not often you let everyone into your humble abode." Josh lifted his beer as a toast, smirking.

"No reason. Just felt the need for a party so I made it happen. Don't fancy the clean-up in the morning, though," he groaned.

"Huh, why not get someone to do it for you?" asked Tate.

"Maybe you could ask the cheerleading squad to help!" laughed his mate.

They both burst into fits of laughter, while Josh and Kent looked at each other and raised their eyebrows; apparently, these two had started the party early. Josh broke eye contact and swung around to scan the open-plan rooms. He saw a beauty across the hall, talking with a girl, and he watched, not at all discreetly, from where he was. Slight build, shoulder-length brown hair and full red lips. He might be a nice distraction. Josh caught his eye as the guy's gaze roamed the area, and Josh smiled, raising his beer in a toast. He had no idea if he was even gay, but he was willing to try. The guy smiled and blushed a deep red. *Goddamn blushes get him every time.*

He pushed away from the counter and started a slow walk to him, occasionally saying hello to friends he passed but keeping eye contact as much as he could.

As he reached him, he vaguely noticed the guy's friend disappear. "Hey," he said, stepping to the side his friend vacated.

He blushed again to Josh's amusement. "Hi," he said as he tucked his hair around his ear.

Josh held his hand out. "I'm Josh. What's your name?" He never went for chat up lines when meeting someone because he was a firm believer that you can be nice and still get your point across.

He shook his hand gently. "Ian."

"Nice to meet you, Ian. Would you like a drink?"

"Um, thanks."

"Follow me, and we'll see what there is." He grabbed Ian's hand carefully, trying not to spook him, and took him back to the kitchen. At the counter, he let go of Ian's hand but rested it on his lower back instead. "See anything you like?" he asked.

Ian looked at the bottles. "I'll have a vodka and coke, please," he said, only loud enough to be heard over the music.

"Coming right up." Josh grabbed the bottles and mixed a drink right in front of him. He didn't want Ian worrying he was doctoring it. "Here you go." He passed it to him.

They spent the next few minutes getting to know each other over their drinks before a shout drew his attention.

"Where is the asshole?" Josh saw people moving out of the way as the person drew closer. "Where the fuck is he?" With that second shout, he realised who it was and rolled his eyes. Why can't he leave it alone? He'd been enjoying his night.

Aiden stopped right in front of him, hands on hips, snarl on his face. "What are you doing here with this bitch?" he spat, giving a dirty once-over at Ian.

"Woah, hang on a minute. There's no need to talk to him like that." Josh stood straight, towering over Aiden. He didn't do this to anyone very often; he hated intimidating them with his size, but Aiden knew exactly how to push his buttons. "He's not done anything to you."

"He's hanging on to my boyfriend. What more does he have to do?" He saw Ian flick a glance to him, hurt on his face.

"Aiden, I told you we were finished two days ago. Remember our conversation earlier, where I told you I knew about Seb? Remember? Yeah, well, that means we're no longer together." Yes, okay, he did sound a little patronising in the speech but what did Aiden expect? He put his beer down on the counter and looked at Ian. "Ian, I'm sorry about this. I really am not with him anymore." Josh was hoping to alleviate his worries, but Ian was looking back and forth between him and Aiden as if debating getting in between them. *Fuck!*

"Just run along, little Ian, and leave Josh to me. Thanks. Bye now!" Aiden waved Ian away from the conversation, even when Josh didn't want him to leave.

"Jesus Christ, Aiden, will you get with the programme! How many more times do I have to tell you we're done?" He threw up his hands and noticed Ian had gone. "Why the hell are you even bothered about me? You've been with someone else. How am I to know you haven't been with more?" Josh looked around the room as he said it, noticing at least two guys who turned their gazes away from him. Shit, obviously more than one.

"You're mine, Josh. No one else can have you." Aiden said in such a sickly sweet, gentle voice it immediately made his spine crawl. How the hell had he not known he was crazy?

"No, Aiden, I'm not and never will be. Kent, I'm out of here. Thanks for the invite." Josh hustled out of the house as quickly as the crowds would let him and almost ran to his car. He wanted to get away from there before Aiden tried anything else. What a nightmare.

5

Charlie

Two days later, Charlie stood before the full-length mirror in his room, looking at his body in his small briefs. Turning from side to side, he tried not to make wardrobe decisions based on the fact Josh was going with him to work today. He'd had a shower and tried to go for his usual black trousers and white shirt, but his fingers strayed to his tight black jeans instead. He knew in his head he shouldn't encourage this thing between them, but his heart was telling him differently.

They had managed a truce of sorts over the past few days. They hadn't flinched when they had accidentally touched and neither had left the room when the other had entered. They weren't talking as easily as before, but he was sure they would get back to being themselves eventually.

He tore the skinny jeans off the shelf and started to put them on before he changed his mind again. He had one leg in when the door opened unexpectedly.

"Would I be okay wearing these jeans—" Josh stopped when he walked into the room, mouth open as he looked at him.

Charlie grabbed for his discarded towel to cover himself. "Shit, Josh." He covered his front with the towel one-handed while he kept hold of the jeans with the other. "Maybe we need to start knocking before entering each other's rooms now?" He blushed as he realised Josh was staring at his reflection in the mirror, which showed his barely covered ass. "Josh!"

Josh moved his eyes down Charlie's reflection one last time before slowly meeting his eyes. He reached behind him to push the door closed without removing his gaze.

"Josh?" Charlie couldn't look away from him. Josh stalked towards him, and Charlie walked backwards away from him. "No, you have to get out of here!" He had no hands to put out in protest. Josh kept walking forward as if he hadn't heard his words. And maybe he hadn't. The back of his knees reached the bed, and he almost tumbled down on to it. "Josh, stop. We can't." Charlie half-heartedly pleaded with Josh, knowing he wasn't being very convincing.

Josh reached out and gently pulled the towel, slowly removing it from his grip and baring Charlie to his eyes. Charlie heard his breath catch. Josh's gaze roamed freely along his body, and he dropped the towel to the floor, reaching a hand forward again. This time, one finger gently traced along his collarbone, making his eyes close and his breathing deepen. The finger followed the trail between his nipples and down to his navel before following the line of his underwear across his stomach.

By this point, Charlie was panting like he had run a marathon, but he never wanted it to stop. Josh retraced his path, bringing his finger back up his chest before cupping Charlie's jaw in his palm.

Charlie opened his eyes and saw the apology before Josh stepped closer.

"I'm sorry..." was all Josh got out before his mouth claimed Charlie's. There was no slow start this time. Josh demanded Charlie accept him, and he could do nothing to deny him. He took Charlie's mouth and his breath for several long minutes. Then he pulled back, gasping when he rested his forehead on his. "I'm sorry, but I have to..." Again, he didn't get a sentence out before he was kissing him again and pushing him gently back on the bed.

Towel and jeans forgotten, Charlie laid back with Josh on top of him, feeling like everything had finally clicked into place. Charlie's heart skipped a beat with the thought, but it was soon flying away along with everything else.

Josh's hand brushed down Charlie's chest, coming to rest on one of his pecs. His whole hand covered one side, squeezing gently, then his thumb grazed his nipple. He rubbed it repeatedly until it budded, then used his thumb and forefinger to roll. The sensation went straight to Charlie's cock, even more so when Josh scraped his nail across the nub. Charlie moaned his pleasure into Josh's mouth, even as Josh's other hand moved further down his body.

In the back of his mind, he realised he had parted his legs for Josh, allowing their erections to press together. Josh's hand smoothed down his side to his jeans and was pulling them off his leg, freeing him from them. His hand was moving up the back of his thigh, pulling him closer to his body.

Charlie's lower body obeyed, and he lifted his pelvis, pushing against Josh. He groaned into Josh's mouth then tore away. Both gasping for breath, Josh began kissing his way down his body, following the path his finger had taken not so long ago. When Josh got to his nipples, he looked up at Charlie, keeping eye contact as he opened his mouth and licked.

Pleasure streamed down to his cock, and he couldn't keep his eyes open as Josh began sucking his nipple into his mouth with strong pulls. As he pulled, his tongue lashed at the nub, creating a dual effect in his stomach and groin. One hand fisted in Josh's hair, pulling him closer while simultaneously pushing him away. He had never felt anything like it before. Josh's other hand coasted over his cock, and Charlie bucked under him, dislodging his mouth.

Josh ran his finger over Charlie's covered cock again, making him arch and cry out his name. Hearing his name must have done something to Josh because he seemed to lose his patience all at once. His mouth moved down his stomach to Charlie's briefs, licking along the waistline before grabbing at it with his teeth. Josh's hands pulled, trying to remove them quickly before stopping suddenly when they got to his knees. Josh leaned his face into them and breathed deep, closing his eyes in pleasure.

Then Josh was frantically pulling them off and rested back in position with his mouth close to his cock. Charlie whimpered and tried to close his legs. He was embarrassed about Josh being down there. He had read books and seen porn about men loving to taste a man, but he had never quite believed it was true. He didn't want Josh doing this if he didn't want to.

"Josh, you don't have to..." he tried to tell him.

Josh growled at him, locking eyes with him before pulling his legs open again. As he had before, he didn't lose eye contact with Charlie as he went in for his first taste. Josh's arms were under Charlie's legs with his hands holding Charlie's hips as he licked across the tip of his cock. Flicking his tongue across the small slit drew murmurs, but when Josh licked the underside, Charlie bowed off the bed. That highly sensitive bundle of nerves shot pleasure throughout his body.

"Holy shit!" Josh chuckled but kept at it until Charlie was incoherent and his hands were fisted in the duvet.

Josh's hands tightened briefly on Charlie's hips before his lips began more torture. Josh licked his whole length from the base to the tip, repeatedly, getting him nice and wet. Then his hand circled the base Charlie's cock, not quite holding hard enough to make him come then draw the head into his mouth with gentle suction.

Josh moved one hand down to Charlie's balls, smoothing his fingers over them, before cupping them and squeezing lightly.

Josh pulled off and blew on Charlie's cock, making him shudder. Josh engulfed the cock completely in his mouth, making him elicit keening sounds he was sure had never heard come out of his own mouth. After several minutes of this, Charlie grabbed Josh's hair and pushed his face against his cock, silently asking for more.

Josh moved his hand up and down tighter, running his tongue under the hood one more time. Charlie bucked up, wanting more wet heat, and Josh began to move his mouth up and down in time with his hand, making sure to suck as he lifted. As Charlie felt his orgasm climb, Josh added a finger pressure to Charlie's hole, flicking his tongue over the head every time he reached the tip. Charlie's grip tightened on his hair, and he cried out Josh's name again.

Josh pressed his finger in little circles, stimulating it more. As Charlie arched in response, Josh drew hard and kept the pressure going until he entered slightly. Charlie went ridged, finally giving in to the orgasm. Josh kept the pressure going, swallowing every bit until Charlie sagged on the bed and pushed against his head to move him away.

"Holy fuck!" Charlie gasped, breathing ragged.

6

Josh

H e rested his forehead against Charlie's pelvis and breathed him in. He was magnificent. Josh couldn't believe he had just done that. Charlie was running his hands through Josh's hair as if he knew he needed a minute. Josh lifted his head and kissed his tip, removing his finger from his ass, making Charlie hiss through his teeth. Then Josh braced himself to look at Charlie.

They were still tangled up. Josh was on the floor beside Charlie's bed, with one arm around his legs and across his stomach and his other framing his cock. Charlie was laid splayed out on the bed, legs apart, a glow on his face.

"You're beautiful," Josh told him. Charlie blushed but didn't move or look away. Josh didn't want to leave this position, but he knew they needed to get ready to go to the bar. "Thank you." He kissed his pelvis before moving his arms and repositioning Charlie's legs. As he stood, Charlie glanced at his trousers and lifted an eyebrow at the bulge.

Josh blushed again. "I'm fine." He smiled and moved over him. He gently pressed some of his weight on Charlie, the rest on his elbows, and kissed his mouth while gazing at him. He didn't usually keep his eyes open when he kissed, but he wanted to see him. Wanted Charlie to see him. The kiss was gentle, coaxing and an apology all in one. He wouldn't say sorry again because Charlie knew, but Josh told him with his mouth.

After another minute, Josh lifted off and pulled Charlie to sitting. He picked up his briefs, passing them over. "You look good in them." Charlie looked up at Josh as he gripped them, and Josh could see the thoughts going around his head. He leaned down and kissed him once then turned to go.

As he got to the door, Charlie called his name. "Jeans will be fine," he said, answering Josh's earlier question with a small smile.

He walked back into his room, pushing the door closed and leaning back against it. He blew out a breath, eyes on the ceiling, his emotions all over the place. He was floored Charlie had been so willing for him, ecstatic for the opportunity, pissed at himself for caving and nervous he now had to spend the next few hours by his side. He could feel his stomach churning; he wasn't sure from which emotion or all of them. He blew out another breath, pressing his palm against his erection, willing it to go down and pushed off from the door. Jeans, it is then. Josh reached into his wardrobe and searched through some tops. Mind still reeling, he pulled out a black and white t-shirt and pulled it on. Running his hands through his hair, he decided this was the best he was going to look. He sat on his bed, reaching for his trainers, wincing when his cock protested. It better go down soon, or he was in trouble. Shoes on, he stood, arms reaching to the ceiling to release some tension. It was going to be a long few hours.

• • • ● • ● • • •

Josh was finished at the bar by ten. It hadn't been as bad as he was expecting; although to begin with he was aware of every single movement Charlie had made, but when Josh concentrated on what Charlie was explaining, the time flew. He'd spent the last three hours learning about drinks, bar service, waitress service and many other things relating to bar work. And as much as he had originally thought he'd hate it, he had enjoyed it. He could see why Charlie had so much fun there.

When he got home, he immediately heard raised voices as he entered. Normally, he would shout out a greeting, but he was curious as to what was going on. He couldn't remember the last time he'd heard his parents arguing. He closed the front door quietly and walked towards the kitchen, trying to keep from view.

"—knew we should have told them before now! We have to say something before they find out some other way!" his mum shouted.

"Helen, how can we explain this to them now, after all these years? Oh, by the way, your Mum and I have been separated for the past three years? Huh, how do you think they're going to take that?" Josh heard Dad slam his hand down, which covered Josh's gasp. He stood there, frozen, not hearing another word being said in the kitchen. Separated? What were they talking about? His mind numb, he didn't see Mum come through the door until she cried out, a hand covering her mouth.

"Josh! Oh, God! I'm so sorry!" She came towards him as if to embrace him, but he finally came back to himself and moved away, hands outstretched. She flinched but didn't come any closer, her shoulders slumping. "You heard." Not a question.

Josh nodded slowly, unable to speak. Dad came up behind her, eyes bleak. "Josh, we're sorry. We didn't want to—"

"Enough." Josh sliced his hand through the air, breathing erratically. "I'm going to bed." He turned and ran up the stairs.

"Josh, wait, please!" Mum called.

"Helen, leave him for now," Dad said, quietly. "We'll talk to him later. We need—"

Josh didn't hear any more as he slammed his door shut. He threw himself on the bed, looking up at the ceiling, mind completely blown.

What the hell was going on? How could that be true? There was no way they could have kept this from them for all this time, but they also wouldn't joke about something this serious. If they were joking, it was so not fucking funny! He brushed his hands over his face, repeatedly, trying to make sense of it all.

He didn't know how long he'd been there, but he shot upright when he heard Charlie coming through the front door with a greeting. He heard mumbling and noises in the kitchen. What was he going to do? Did he tell Charlie? Did he keep their secret for them? He didn't know what to do. Josh swung his legs over the edge of the bed and began biting his nails. He heard footsteps coming up the stairs, then a soft knock on his door.

"Yeah," he rasped, voice hoarse, not sure who he wanted it to be.

"Can I come in?" Charlie's voice whispered through.

"Uh-huh." He didn't trust his voice again.

Charlie entered, stopping inside and cocked his head to the side. "Mum said you weren't feeling very good. You were okay earlier. What happened?"

Josh stared at him for a moment before realising he couldn't keep this from him. If for no other reason than he needed someone to talk to about it. Which was selfish, but he also deserved to know.

"Come in and close the door," he whispered, not moving from his spot on the bed.

Charlie hesitated briefly, but Josh obviously looked as wrecked as he felt because he did as asked. Charlie moved closer, stopping an arms width away. "What's wrong?"

Josh didn't think about his reaction but grabbed Charlie's wrist, dragging him towards him. Charlie gasped a protest, but it didn't stop Josh from lying him on his bed and spooning him from behind before he could react any further.

"Josh," he whispered, "what are you doing? Mum and Dad might come in." He wriggled as if to move from his position, but Josh wrapped an arm around his waist and pressed his face into Charlie's neck. After a brief hesitation, Charlie's hands covered his. "You're scaring me. What's happened? Please tell me!" His voice shook, which brought Josh out of his own thoughts.

He tightened his hands and began talking. "I have something to say which is going to upset you, and although I don't want to, I can't keep it from you," he mumbled, breathing onto Charlie's neck.

"Tell me," Charlie ordered firmly. "It can't be any worse than the thoughts going through my head right now. You're really worrying me, Josh." His voice trembled, his breathing coming fast and harsh.

"Shhh, it's okay. Okay, I'm telling you, and I'm sorry in advance," Josh warned him. "Mum and Dad are separated and have been for three years."

Josh held his breath. As Charlie lay in silence, Josh's mind flipped through scene after scene of their parents, happy, kissing, touching, generally being happily married. And together. How can they be separated? It doesn't make sense. He came back to the present, realised Charlie was crying soundlessly. He wrapped Charlie tighter in his arms, one arm up across his chest to his shoulder, the other across his waist still holding him tight.

"It's okay, it's okay, you're fine. Stay with me, Charlie. I'm right here. I'm sorry. So sorry, Charlie. I'm sorry I had to tell you. Please forgive me." Josh's voice was quiet but wet from tears. Charlie reached his hands to Josh's and squeezed briefly, then encouraged him to let go. "Please don't go, Charlie. I'm so—"

"Shh, let me turn around," Charlie whispered. Josh finally released him enough that Charlie could wiggle onto his other side to look at him. He looked wrecked. He reached his hands up and wiped the tears from Charlie's face. Catching his breath, Charlie said, "You have nothing to be sorry for. Thank you for telling me. And thank you for being here when I found out." He blew out a deep breath into Josh's chest. Josh's arms tightened briefly around his waist and Charlie rested his forehead against Josh's, breathing slowly. "It's mind-blowing!" he said with a little laugh. Charlie lifted his head again, looking Josh in the eye. "We'll be fine."

There was a knock on his door. "Josh, can we talk, honey?" Mum's voice came through the door. Josh felt Charlie tense and tightened his arms, stopping Charlie from moving.

Voice hard, Josh replied. "No, we can't. I'm talking with Charlie. I'll talk to you tomorrow." He was harsh with his words, but even he could hear the pain beneath them. Charlie reached his arms around to Josh's back and held him tight, resting his head against Josh's chest under his chin.

"Oh. Well, okay," she said hesitantly, then more quietly but loud enough for them to hear. "I'm assuming you've told him. All I can say is I'm so sorry, both of you. We should have told you sooner. We didn't want to hurt you—" she broke off with a sob. Josh could hear the tears in her voice, and although he was worried about his mother, he was more worried about Charlie at the moment. He was so tense Josh was worried he'd snap. He heard their mother leave and snuggled closer.

After a while, they manoeuvred so Josh was lying on his back and Charlie was cuddled up against his side, head resting on his chest, arm across his waist, hand linked with his. Josh ran his other hand through his hair repeatedly. There was silence between them, but it was comforting in the face of such uncertainty.

· · · ● · ● · ● · · ·

Waking slowly, Josh smelled vanilla and took a deep breath. He became more alert after memories of the previous evening intruded, and he realised he was cuddled up with something warm and deliciously scented. Make that *someone*. His now wide-awake brain registered the fact he was spooned against Charlie's back, arm around his waist, fingers linked, head in his hair. Basically, as close as you could get to another person. He took another slow deep breath, stealing another moment before real life interrupted. Reality intruded when Josh realised his morning wood was nestled right against Charlie's ass.

Shit, he thought, holding his breath and trying to decide what to do. Should he move and risk waking Charlie or should Josh stay where he was and feign sleep until he wakes? Indecision lost him time, and Charlie began to move softly, pressing his ass further against Josh's cock, making him bite back a moan. Charlie settled again but only after moving their linked hands to the top of his trousers. Josh closed his eyes and held his breath again, hoping Charlie stopped moving before Josh lost his non-existent control.

Last night, Charlie had only left him to get changed from his work clothes into pyjama trousers, then came back and settled next to Josh again, talking long into the night. That meant this morning, the only thing between them was Charlie's thin trousers and his cotton ones. Nothing strong enough to keep from showing Josh's arousal.

"Mmm," Charlie murmured as he began to move again. Charlie moved his left hand from under his cheek, resting it across his stomach, while his right hand, linked as it was with his, began to move further down, between Charlie's legs. Josh was still in two minds. Charlie appeared to be dreaming so Josh wondered if he could remove himself discreetly so Charlie could continue alone. Josh wanted to stay, but he was unsure if Charlie would freak out when he woke and realised Josh was there. "Mmm, Josh," Charlie mumbled.

It was *his* name Charlie said, so Josh decided he'd stay and deal with the fallout after. Mind made up, he allowed Charlie to lead the way. He lifted his head slowly to watch Charlie.

Josh tried to keep his breathing even when Charlie pressed their loosely joined hands under Charlie's trousers, wrapping their fingers around his erect cock. Charlie's left hand moved to flick slowly over his own nipple, making it bead. Josh's breath caught at the sight, his mind already on what it would feel like in his mouth. Charlie arched into their hands, sighing at the firmer contact.

Josh was hardly breathing, not daring to move too much himself, scared if he did Charlie would stop but also scared he wouldn't. Josh's mind was telling him to stop this before it went too far again, but his heart and body were happy to tag along for the ride. If their parents found them like this... Josh turned his mind away from the thought and back to where his hand was. Charlie opened his legs wider and moved their hands up and down his shaft. Josh wasn't sure how Charlie was still asleep because it must be strange jacking off while holding hands. Josh knew it felt a little strange from his side.

Josh gasped as he felt the precome; Charlie was dripping everywhere. He could feel the wetness of Charlie's trousers on the back of his hand. The fingers on Charlie's nipple was thrumming faster and squeezing in time with their hands on his cock as they stroked rhythmically. Josh was struggling with restraint now and wasn't sure how much longer he could hold back. Then Charlie cried out, and that was it: Josh was lost.

He released their joined hands, moving his precome covered hand frantically over Charlie's mouth to stop the cry from leaving of the room. Charlie jerked awake, moving his head to look at Josh over his shoulder. He saw Charlie blush bright red, realisation dawning in his widening eyes, then his nostrils flared, and his eyes grew heavy with desire. Josh realised Charlie could smell the scent on Josh's fingers, so after tightening his fingers to tell Charlie to be quiet, he slipped his fingers into Charlie's mouth. Eyes closing, Charlie groaned quietly as he sucked and licked Josh's fingers clean, while still strumming at his nipple.

Josh allowed him to lick the remnants off, then slowly removed his fingers from Charlie's mouth. He moved up onto his elbow for better access and turned Charlie onto his back to face him, kissing him hard. Keeping his mouth on Charlie's, Josh smoothed his hand along his arm and wrist until Josh took over from where Charlie's hand was still stroking his cock. Sliding Charlie's fingers off, Josh swirled his fingers to surround his cock, pumping slowly.

"Fuck, you're so hot," he gasped against his lips. His hand tightened and pumped faster, with his tongue copying the motions. Breaking away from Charlie's mouth, he tongued his neck.

"God, Josh! I'm gonna come!" Charlie whispered raggedly. Josh kept up the pace, stroking his hand up and down as fast as he could. Josh saw Charlie frantically squeezing and flicking his nipple, his hand gripping Josh's wrist tightly while Josh jerked him off. Swiping his finger over the tip of Charlie's cock, Josh jammed his mouth over Charlie's as he came, swallowing his cry. The feeling of Charlie's come covering his hand had him pressing his cock against Charlie's hip for friction.

Josh gentled the kiss until they were resting their lips against each other's, breathing erratically. He slowed his hand some but still moved up and down until Charlie's hand pushed his away, telling him it was too sensitive. Removing his hand completely, Josh lifted them to his mouth and sucked them clean. Charlie's taste burst over his tongue as it had last time. He was sure the taste would never get old.

"Fuck, that is so hot!" Charlie whimpered, gaze on Josh's mouth. He looked well satisfied but Josh was still hard as stone. He went to move so he could deal with it in the shower when Charlie grabbed his arm, stopping him from going anywhere. Charlie blushed, not quite meeting his eyes. "Can I...." he bit his lip, before continuing, "Can I help you?" he asked quietly.

Josh's eyes closed briefly, then he tilted Charlie's chin up to see his eyes. He needed to check Charlie was okay with this. "You sure?" he asked, waiting to see an answer in his eyes.

He nodded, pinking up again. "Yes."

Taking a breath, Josh moved to lay on his back. "Wait," Charlie said, stopping him again. "Can you be over me?" Josh looked at him again, then moved Charlie onto his back before straddling his legs. "Hang on." Charlie wriggled his legs out from between his so Josh could settle between, still on his knees but with Charlie's legs bracketing his groin. As if they were about to make love.

With a groan, Josh rested his weight between his knees and his forearms as he closed in on Charlie and kissed him. Tongues duelling, he felt Charlie's hands drag down his chest and abs, heading for his waistband. Charlie played with the band for a minute until Josh growled and slid his hand underneath. Charlie gasped into his mouth as he touched Josh's cock. Josh groaned. "Fuck, Charlie." Josh couldn't stop his hips from bucking, especially as Charlie closed his hand around him. Squeezing gently, Charlie slid his hand up and down Josh's shaft. Josh thought he would explode in seconds. Managing to hold off, he allowed Charlie the chance to experiment and explore. He refused to push Charlie before he was ready. But it might kill him in the process.

Resting his forehead against Charlie's pecs, Josh panted heavily against his skin. "Oh God, fuck, that feels so good." He knew he wasn't going to last long, especially when Charlie asked to watch. "Huh?" His brain had no blood in it, so it took a minute for him to understand, especially as Charlie was still stroking him. Josh lifted his head to look at him.

"Can I watch you come?" Charlie asked again. "I want to see." Josh could see Charlie was turned on, the flush in his cheeks spreading to his chest.

"Oh God, Charlie." Josh groaned again as he lifted onto his hands, elbows locked so there was space between them for Charlie to see. Charlie used his other hand to push Josh's trousers under his cock and ass, giving him the perfect view. Josh watched Charlie's eyes widen and his tongue wet his kiss bruised lips.

"Fuck, Charlie. I'm not gonna last much longer!" He began to rock his hips, in time with Charlie's movements, gaining more friction. "Ah, shit!" He was gasping now, even though Josh was trying to keep quiet. His hips moved faster as Charlie tightened his grip. "Fuck, I'm coming! I'm coming!" His breath stuttered.

Ropes of his come splashed across Charlie's stomach as he kept up his stroking. Josh came harder than he ever remembered coming before. His arms let him down, and he fell to his elbows, breathing hard onto Charlie's chest as he rested his forehead. "Fuck, Charlie. Fuck." Josh was completely dazed and worn out.

Removing his hand, Charlie started giggling. Josh lifted his forehead, playfully frowning at him. "Why are you laughing at a time like this?"

Charlie tried to get himself under control. "I can't believe we did that with Mum and Dad in the house!" he said, trying to keep quiet.

Josh burst out laughing too. He'd never had that experience before. Laughter with sex was not something he would have thought about before, but it seemed so natural with Charlie.

The laughter subsided after a minute and Josh looked at him. He saw confusion in Charlie's eyes, which he was sure was reflected in his. He pressed their lips together gently. "We'll sort it out. Try not to worry." He kissed Charlie again and lifted off him. "We best get cleaned up." Josh got off the bed and held out his hands. Charlie reached out for him and let Josh help him up, squeezing his hand as they separated. "You go shower first. I'll see you in a bit."

Josh didn't want things getting awkward again, so he tried to act normally. Charlie gave a small smile and walked to the door. Turning back, Charlie looked at him. "Thank you," he said quietly and went out of the room, closing Josh's door behind him.

7

Charlie

C harlie entered the bathroom, locking the door behind him and sat on the toilet seat. Resting his elbows on his knees, he covered his mouth with one hand, staring blankly at the floor. *Oh my God, that was the hottest thing ever!* He blushed even as his mouth turned up into a grin. *I can't believe that happened!* He bit his lip trying to keep his laughter quiet and pushed his hands through his hair, blowing out a breath to calm down.

Charlie turned the water on and stripped off, feeling the slight tackiness between his legs. He closed his eyes again, remembering the feeling of having Josh's fingers on him. He wasn't naïve, he knew most cocks were bigger than Josh's fingers, so he could imagine how much he would ache after sex; he hoped it would be a nice ache though.

Ducking under the water, he cleaned his hair and body, butterflies still swarming in his stomach.

"Charlie! Where are you?" Mum's voice doused him with cold water, even though the shower was hot enough to steam.

"Fuck!" he whispered. "In the shower, Mum! I'll be down in a minute!" he yelled above the sound of the water. He rested his head against the tiles. "Fuck, fuck, fuck, shit, damn!" They couldn't keep doing this, especially in the same house as their parents. It was so wrong; society would string them up if it were to get out.

But why, oh why, did it feel completely right? Every time he was with Josh, he felt complete. Charlie had never been a fairy tale ending type of person usually, but those were the thoughts and feelings that went through him every time they were together.

He wasn't going to find answers in the shower. Turning off the shower and towelling dry, he tied the towel around his waist. He picked up his clothes and opened the bathroom door.

"All yours, Josh!" he shouted, trying to keep his voice normal as he walked to his own room.

Shutting the door behind him, he leaned against it for a moment, then strode over and dropped onto the bed. He sat there staring at the floor before rubbing his hands over his face before standing and crossing to his wardrobe. He held the doors open and stared at the clothes. He felt, kind of, numb now. Thoughts were swirling in his head, but he couldn't get one particular thought to emerge coherently. Finally, he gave up and picked out some clothes. He was working until close today so didn't have to be at work until six. A free day would do him good.

Grabbing his phone, he messaged Ginny and asked if she wanted to go shopping. Within ten minutes, they'd arranged to meet at the shopping centre, have lunch and do some window shopping. He'd not seen her for about a week, so it would be nice to catch up. Charlie went about getting himself ready and skipped down the stairs for breakfast.

Walking into the kitchen was like walking into a funeral. Mum and Dad were sat at the table nursing mugs of coffee and Josh was stood by the toaster, staring out the window in silence. All at once, Charlie remembered what had happened yesterday. How could he have forgotten?

"Morning," he said quietly, heading over to Josh. Putting his hand against Josh's spine, Josh jumped slightly. "Sorry. Do you want some toast?" he asked, gently.

Josh blinked at him for a moment, then shook his head. "No, thanks," he said, turning his attention back to outside. Charlie put his head against his upper arm briefly, then moved away to get the bread for his toast. He wasn't quite sure how to act with his parents because in reality, although he and Josh had spoken about it last night, he still hadn't got it completely straight in his head.

"Are you at college today?" he asked Josh, pushing the lever on the toaster.

"Um, yeah, long day today, so I'll be back before five," he said, turning to face him.

"Okay, I might see you for a few minutes before I head to work." The toast popped up, and Josh plated it and handed it to him. "Thanks." He grabbed the butter from the fridge. "I'm heading out after breakfast to meet with Ginny. I'm trying to get in some socialising before work tonight." He aimed the remark at his parents, though kept his eyes on his food.

No one said anything for a moment until his mum said, "That's nice, sweetheart. Have a lovely time."

"Helen, we—" Dad started.

"No, John. We will talk when they're ready and not before." Charlie looked around and saw his mother placing her hand on his father's wrist. "Give them time, darling." She patted his wrist, then coiled it around her mug again.

Dad looked over at him and Josh, mouth in a thin line but gave a small nod and went back to looking at the table.

Well this isn't awkward at all, is it, Charlie? he thought. Finishing the toast, he placed the plate in the dishwasher. "Right, I'm heading off. I should be back for about two unless we decide to make a day of it. If we do, it will be around four. See you later." He gave his parents a little wave and smile, looked at Josh and walked back to his room.

Heaving a huge sigh, he put on his boots and grabbed his coat, making sure his wallet and phone were in his pockets. Shoving it over his shoulder, he made his way back downstairs. Josh was leaving the kitchen, head down.

"Hey," he said, stopping in front of him. "It'll be fine, regardless of what happens, we still have us. We're still going to be here for each other, okay?" He reached his arms around Josh's neck and kissed his cheek, giving him a squeeze. "We'll be fine," he stated firmly. Then he turned and left the house.

• • • ● ● • ● ● • • •

Watching Ginny walk into the café was like watching a wave caress the shoreline. She made people smile just by walking past them. She was taller than Charlie by a few inches and had the confidence to walk the walk. Perfectly tousled, auburn hair rested at her shoulders while framing an oval, pale-skinned face with green eyes and rosy lips. Charlie often wondered how he managed to find friends who could easily pass for supermodels, whereas he was a normal skinny, brown-haired guy. But the main thing was they didn't act like supermodels, so as far as he was concerned that was an extra point in their favour.

Ginny waved to several people on the way to where Charlie was sitting, smiling with her entire mouth, which always lit up her face. Charlie was so jealous of those teeth. She would be happy to swap mouths if it was ever a possibility because she hated them—said there were too many teeth which made her look like a dental commercial. Charlie loved them and had told Ginny several times it showed her genuine happiness about people surrounding her. She'd only grumbled under her breath after that.

"Hey, Charlie Bear! How you been?" Ginny sat down at the table, placing her bag on the floor beside her. Charlie hated being called that, but that was why she did it. She wasn't being mean; she was just being annoying.

"Shut up! And alright, I suppose. I do have a few things to tell you."

Ginny looked at him, her eyes widening in anticipation. "You don't usually have much out of the ordinary to tell me. So, what's going on?" Ginny gushed, so excited by the prospect of gossip.

"Slow down, slow down!" Charlie raised his hands in a calming gesture.

Charlie rose to get their order, a coffee and muffin for him, mint tea and scone for Ginny and returned to the table to start in on the first news of the day.

"So, I might have made an arrangement to meet up with Jimmy one night, and it backfired on me," Charlie said before quickly filling his mouth with muffin so he couldn't give her any more information. He also knew Ginny needed to let her mouth run away for a while before she would calm.

And true to form, Ginny dropped her scone back down. "What the fuck were you thinking, Charlie? Jimmy? Oh, of all people why did you have to choose him? Flipping heck, boy, you need your mind checked. Jimmy! There are plenty of other people you can choose from! What in the world made you go to him? Bloody hell, I need more than tea for this conversation I think." Ginny huffed and grabbed her tea, spilling some on the table.

Grabbing a napkin, Charlie tried to explain his reasoning in a quiet voice. "You know I'm still a virgin, Gin. I honestly thought it would be a win-win scenario. He would get what he has been after for years, and I would lose my virginity. Hey, presto! Problem solved." Charlie threw his hands in the air. "But I forgot how much of an asshole he really is." Charlie slumped in his seat, fiddling with the mug handle. Maybe he needed something stronger than coffee too.

"Bloody hell." She huffed again, then sat back and looked at Charlie. Quietly, she asked, "Are you okay?"

Charlie looked at her with gratitude. "Yeah, I'm okay. Sore pride more than anything."

Ginny grabbed Charlie's hand and squeezed. "Tell me what happened."

Charlie explained what happened four nights prior. When he was finished, he waited for the explosion again. Instead, he saw tears in her eyes.

"Ginny, what's wrong?" Charlie grabbed her hands and rubbed.

"I'm thinking of what could have happened. God, Charlie, no one knew what you were doing. Jimmy could have raped you for God's sake and no one would have known." Ginny gasped as she spoke, and Charlie had a sudden realisation. He thought he knew Jimmy, knew his personality, knew his behaviour. But, yes, he had very much been in danger of that happening. And he hadn't thought about his safety walking home alone after either. Charlie's heart rate increased before he calmed again, reminding himself he was fine and nothing had happened.

In all honesty, he was still waiting to find out the repercussions of refusing Jimmy. He told her as much.

"Something will come of it, I'm sure. Jimmy is not known to go quietly, especially as I'm sure he had bragged to his friends about it beforehand." She stared at Charlie. "Be careful, Charlie. I don't like Jimmy one bit, and I don't want this coming back to bite you in the ass."

"I will." Charlie squeezed her hand one more time before leaning back to eat some more of his muffin.

"How was Josh?"

Charlie coughed up his bite of the muffin when Ginny's question registered. He took a drink of coffee to help clear it. "What?"

Charlie looked at her, eyes wide, scared they'd been found out. How had she known?

"You messaged me about teaching him to bartend. How did it go? Was he any good?" She looked at him with a frown. "Was he awful?"

"Oh yeah, he was good." *He was definitely good.* Charlie took another sip of coffee, allowing himself a moment to calm his thoughts. Fuck! His heart was racing! "He was good. He picked it up fast, surprisingly. Especially as he said he had no interest in doing it. Before he left, he said he'd like to learn more."

"It would be good for him. He'd have no issues finding a job near uni if he could bartend. There are plenty of places around that need people."

"Yeah, that's what Dad said too." Charlie finished his final bite of muffin and sat back. "Which brings me to news number two."

"Oooh, goodie, more gossip." Ginny leaned forward, arms crossed and resting on the table. "Tell me more," she said with a smile.

"Mum and Dad are separated." Charlie waited for a beat. "And have been for three years." He watched her reaction.

She didn't disappoint. Her mouth dropped open, eyes wide, for once she was struck incoherent. "What-? Why-? How-?" She stopped. "What the actual fuck?"

"Yeah, that pretty much sums it up," Charlie said with a laugh, sipping his coffee.

"I don't even know where to start with that! Flippin' heck, Charlie! How did you find out?"

He wrapped his hands around the mug, trying to warm them, even though he knew the cold feeling was only in his head. "Josh found out. He came back from the bar to hear them arguing about telling us. When I got home, Mum told me Josh was upset and asked me to go see if he was okay. When I went up, he was a wreck, and then told me what he'd heard." Charlie sighed. "I don't know what to do with it all. It's completely come out of the blue. I thought they were happy. They never showed anything other than a united front for us. And to do that while they were separated? It's blown me away, Ginny." He shook his head while staring at the table. "And as for Josh. He's gone to college today, but I don't think he and my parents actually spoke to each other this morning, and I don't know how to help."

Ginny reached forward and rested her hand against Charlie's. "Just be there for him and him for you, which I'm sure he will be." She gave a small smile. "And you need to sit down and talk with your parents. I know it will be tough to hear it all, but you need to find out what happened and what's going to happen now. I'm assuming because it's come out now there is a change about to happen."

That was the other thing about Ginny. She was an all-round nice person, and Charlie knew when she gave advice, it probably should be taken. Even if it seemed like the hardest route. She seemed a lot older and wiser than her nineteen years. Charlie blew out another breath, rubbed his face with his hands and grabbed the coffee again.

"Anyway, have you any news for me?" he asked Ginny, changing the subject. He almost didn't catch her face flushing red. "Ginny? Are you holding out on me?" Charlie said with a chuckle, narrowing his eyes playfully.

"Um..." She straightened in her seat, brushing her hands down her front and not looking at him.

"Ginny, what's going on? You can tell me; you know you can." Charlie cocked his head to the side, trying to figure out if she had good or bad news.

"Well, you see, I've been to Crush a few times over the last few weeks. Um, well you were there sometimes, and...sometimes I went when you weren't." It was Charlie's turn to be speechless now. Not because Ginny had been to the bar without him but because she was stumbling over sentences. She had never been uncomfortable enough to do that before. But for some reason, today she was.

"Okay." Charlie dragged out the word. "That's okay. You are allowed to go there without me." He was fumbling around as he didn't know what her issue was.

"I know. I know. Um, well when I've been there, I've been sat at the bar talking to Analise when she's there and also, um, with Tom." Ginny said the last bit quickly, still not looking at Charlie and fidgeting with the menu instead.

"Ginny, spit it out. You're starting to freak me out." And she was. Charlie had *never* seen her like this before.

"IwentonadatewithTom." She said it in such a rush Charlie had to let his brain process it before he could understand what was said. When he had, he rested back against the chair, staring at her. "I'm so sorry, but he's so nice and kind, and he always talks to me and is really kind, and we kind of hit it off after talking so many times, and when he asked me out, I said yes." She stopped and finally looked at Charlie. "Are you mad at me?" she said quietly.

Charlie burst out laughing, causing people at other tables to turn and look over at them. Ginny covered her face and Charlie realised she didn't understand why. He quickly reached over and pulled her hands away. "Ginny, it's fine, don't worry." Charlie looked her in the face. "You just looked damn cute being so tongue-tied, and I've never seen it before." Charlie laughed again and shook his head. "Wow. I don't know what to say. Have you been on the date yet?"

Ginny nodded. "We went for lunch yesterday."

"And...?"

"I really like him, Charlie," she whispered.

"I can see that." Charlie smiled. "You know he's older than you, don't you?"

Ginny laughed. "Yes, he's nineteen years older than me. It was one of his first concerns, but after talking about loads of different topics while we were at the bar, he told me he'd come to realise it didn't matter unless it mattered to the both of us. When I told him, it didn't matter to me, he asked me out." She smiled widely. Charlie thought she looked so happy at that moment and wished dearly his life was at that point. Don't get him wrong, he was enjoying the brief interludes with Josh but, for god's sake, they were siblings. He knew it was wrong and it would eventually stop. He wished with all his being things were different, but he had to buckle up and realise it wasn't going to happen.

He had no idea what he was going to do about Josh, but at the moment, he didn't think he was strong enough to push him away, especially with everything that was happening at home.

"Charlie, you okay?" Ginny's question interrupted Charlie's thoughts.

"Yes, fine, yeah." He turned back to the conversation.

"You sure you're okay with this? Me and Tom?" She looked anxious.

"Yes. I'm fine so long as you're happy." Charlie tried to reassure her as much as he could. "But I'm telling you now, I am going to have soooo much fun with this." Charlie smirked and laughed as she palmed her face again.

"Oh, God!"

"Yep, you're mine, missy." Charlie laughed as he grabbed his coat and stood. "Come on, let's go window shopping."

• • • ● • ● • • •

Spending a couple of hours looking around the shops with Ginny was just what Charlie needed. Charlie had spent the time alternating between teasing her about Tom and brooding about his situation. Although every time she caught him moping, she made him laugh.

They were looking through the sale clothes when Charlie's mobile rang. Sliding it out of his pocket, he saw Josh was calling.

"Hey, what's up?"

"Charlie. Can you come and get me?" Josh's voice was strained, his words cracking.

"Are you okay?" Charlie asked immediately, many scenarios running through his head. He threw the jacket he was holding back on to the rail and waved his hand to get Ginny's attention.

"No, come get me. Please." His voice broke on the last word.

"Yep, I'm coming. Where are you?" Charlie ran out of the store, trying to get to his car as quick as he could.

"Entrance to college."

"I'm coming. I'm coming." Charlie heard nothing, looked at his phone and realised Josh had hung up. "Ginny, I have to go and get Josh. Will you be okay?" They'd arrived at his car.

"Yes, I'll be fine. Go to him. Ring me later."

"Okay, thanks. I will." Charlie jumped in the car, fastened his belt and started driving towards Josh, wondering what the hell was wrong.

• • • ● • ● • ● • ● • ●

It only took Charlie fifteen minutes to get to him, but it seemed like a lifetime when he didn't know what was wrong. Every red traffic light made his heart stop, thinking he would be too late. But eventually, he squealed to a stop when he saw Josh sat on the path with his back to the stone wall near the college entrance. He wasn't supposed to park there, but right then, he couldn't care less. Charlie opened his door and undid his belt at the same time, leaving the car running and ran to Josh.

"Josh! What's the matter? What happened?" He went to his knees in front of him, using his hands to lift Josh's chin so he could see his face. "Josh?"

Josh lifted his eyes to him, and he watched as Josh crumbled. Charlie grabbed him in his arms and held him as tight as he could while Josh sobbed his heart out. He could feel his top getting wet with Josh's tears and his own began to drip down his cheek. Charlie's heart broke for him. For them both. His brother, so strong, was also just a boy who had been dealt a blow. Josh kept his face hidden in Charlie's neck, probably to avoid the stares of the students who passed them by. He kept up his soothing words and stroking his head and back until Josh seemed to calm.

Charlie was on his knees, cradled in between Josh's legs, with Josh's arms banded around his waist, his around Josh's back and head. He felt as Josh breathed deeply then moved his hands, one up his back and one towards his ass.

"Josh, don't. Not here," Charlie whispered, as he tried to pull back. He stopped trying to get free when Josh tightened his arms but stopped moving them. Charlie looked around them. It must be class time as the paths were pretty much empty, only the odd student here and there.

Josh lifted his head. His eyes were red and wet, but he seemed calmer. Charlie rested his palm against his cheek. "Are you doing okay?" he asked, looking in his eyes.

Before he could stop him, Josh pressed his lips against Charlie's for a few seconds; more than socially acceptable for siblings. Then he pulled away. Charlie was glad Josh had the strength to do it because he didn't think he would have been able to. "Sorry," Josh said as he gathered his bag together and began to stand.

Charlie moved out of his way and climbed to his feet, looking around to see if anyone was paying attention to them. Luckily, he didn't think so. "Come on, let's get you home." Charlie checked his watch. Nearly one. "Or do you want to go out for lunch?"

He watched as Josh hooked his bag on his shoulder and walked towards the car.

Opening the passenger door, Josh looked at him. "Can we go out? I don't want to go home yet."

Charlie nodded and got in the driver's seat. "Shall we go to Pop's?" he asked.

Josh shook his head. "Can we go somewhere further afield? I'd like somewhere people don't know us as well as they do there." Josh threw his bag on the back seat and buckled himself in, resting his hands on his knees.

Charlie thought for a moment and then had an idea of where to go. "No problem. I have just the place." He started driving toward the edge of town.

When they left Cambridge, Josh looked at him. "We could've stayed in town. I didn't mean this far out."

"I know. There's a café just opened in Milton. Thought we'd try it out." Charlie kept his eyes on the road. "That okay?"

"Sure." Josh seemed calmer, even if he kept sighing and rubbing his face.

Charlie pulled into the café car park. Parking the car, he turned the engine off and they studied at The Roadside Café. It looked nice and clean. It had only been open a few months but from what he'd heard from gossip at the bar, the people and food seemed nice. Charlie wasn't sure how busy it would be or how many people they would know, but he had assumed it would be less than at Pop's. Because *everyone* went to Pop's.

Josh held the door open for him, and walking through the entrance, Charlie realised he'd been right. There was no one he recognised sitting at the counter or any of the tables. Leading the way, he grabbed a booth-style table at the back away from the other patrons. He sat down, breathing out wearily and grabbed the menu.

The waitress came over promptly and asked for their drink order. Charlie ordered coffee because he had an inkling he was going to need it. Josh ordered a mocha. They both ordered the all-day breakfast.

After the waitress left, he looked at Josh; he had his hands linked on the table and his eyes were on them. Charlie waited for him to say something. When he didn't, he reached across, covering his hands and squeezing.

"What happened?" he asked quietly.

Josh was silent for a moment. Then he licked his lips, took a breath. "We started a new topic in class. We had to draw or paint emotions." He paused. "They asked us to choose an emotion that felt strong enough to be tangible." He licked his lips again. "All I kept thinking of was the anger I felt." He laughed without humour. "My painting was basically red and black splatters all over the canvas. When the tutor saw, he asked me if I was okay. To which I replied, "No I'm fucking not," and stormed out of the class."

"Oh, Josh." He squeezed Josh's hands again as Josh lent forward to rest his forehead on their joined hands. Charlie moved one of his hands out and rested it on his head, stroking his soft hair. He realised Josh had not put any product in it today, so his hand felt like it was caressing silk. "Josh. I'm so sorry about all this."

Josh sat up again, making Charlie's hand fall away and he grabbed it. "Why are you sorry? You didn't do anything wrong."

"I know, but I hate you hurting."

"You make it better." Josh looked him in the eyes, and Charlie saw things he really should keep locked away.

Charlie looked away, removing his hands as he spied the waitress returning with their drinks.

"Thanks."

"No problem. Lunch will be with you shortly." The waitress left again.

They both wrapped their hands around their mugs, laughing at their mirrored positions. Charlie took a sip, moaning at the taste and the heat of the coffee, then blushed as he realised Josh was staring at him, heat blazing in his eyes. "Stop it," he whispered, tearing his eyes away.

"Sorry." Charlie glanced at him again, seeing he'd returned his gaze to the table. Charlie moved, making himself more comfortable on the seat, crossing his legs at the ankle. It was only when he bumped legs with Josh that he realised how close they were. He stilled then moved to sit how he had been. Before he could, Josh had hooked his feet around his ankles, stopping him from moving away.

Charlie chuckled. "What are we? In school?" he said, looking at him with a smile.

He saw Josh's mouth tilt up then he started chuckling into his mug. After a minute, he stopped and said, "If this is the only way I can show you how much you mean to me when we're in public, so be it." He didn't look at him, though.

Charlie wanted to cry at that point. He was so confused about everything that was going on with them, but he knew for definite things were getting too serious. Soon they wouldn't be able to back away without consequences. It was probably too late already. He closed his eyes, biting his lip and breathing deeply to stop the threat of tears. He didn't want to upset Josh any further. They were both going through so much now; everything seemed to be piling on top of his shoulders.

His eyes shot open when the waitress placed a plate in front of him, making him jump. Luckily, he kept hold of the coffee without spilling. "Um, thanks." He placed the mug on the table and grabbed the cutlery.

8

Josh

J osh kept watching Charlie from under his lashes. He appeared to be on edge, understandably, so Josh backed off. He knew he needed the connection of them at that moment, but if it was making Charlie uncomfortable, he needed to stop. He couldn't seem to make himself pull his legs away but tried to step back with everything else.

"How's Ginny?" he asked, remembering where Charlie had been that morning.

"Oh, she's good." Charlie chuckled. "Got herself a new boyfriend." He smirked.

"That's good. Anyone I know?" Josh began to dig into his food, realising he was starving. The greasiness of it was like a balm to his soul. Nothing beats breakfast at any time of day.

"Tom."

Josh frowned when he couldn't place the name to a face. Then he saw Charlie's face and realised he meant the one 'Tom' he had pushed aside straight away. "Really? Wow. I'd never have thought of those two together. How long have they known each other?"

"Well, they've known each other in passing for as long as I've worked at the bar, obviously. But Ginny had gone when I wasn't there one night and had started a conversation with Tom. Apparently, it went from there, until after some serious conversations about their age difference, Tom asked her out. It's kinda cute."

Josh laughed. "I'm not sure Tom would appreciate being called cute."

"Hey, he can still be cute at thirty-nine!" Charlie defended. "It's not just baby-faced guys that get called that. I always thought he was good looking but not in a romantic kind of way." Charlie ate some bacon but dripped ketchup on his chin. Josh automatically reached a finger forward and wiped it off, putting his finger in his own mouth. Charlie froze, eyes locked on his as he took his finger back out, swallowed and carried on eating his lunch. *Shit, I shouldn't have done that.* Josh squirmed in his chair a little until he heard Charlie go back to eating.

Maybe a public place was not the place to be. Although a private place was probably not the place to be either if they intended to stop what kept happening between them. He swallowed again, then resumed eating.

They finished their lunch, making small talk about college and work, ignoring the two elephants in the room—them and their parents.

"Let's head back home. I think I need some sleep," Josh said, yawning behind his hand. He stood, waiting for Charlie, then went to the cashier to pay.

Walking back to Charlie's car, Josh waited at the passenger door. "Thanks for coming to get me," he said quietly.

Charlie looked at him. "Not a problem at all." He smiled and got in the car. Once Josh was sitting, he pulled out and headed home. He didn't know if he hoped his parents were there or not. He'd deal with it when he got there.

• • • ● • ● • ● • •

Luckily, their parents weren't home, so he was able to go right to his room and sleep. The minute his head hit his pillow, he was gone. When he woke, there was still sunlight coming in his windows, so he knew he'd not slept too long. Looking at his clock, he saw it said three-forty. He'd only slept for about an hour. He rolled to his back and listened for any noise within the house, but he couldn't hear anything and wasn't sure if he wanted company. He laid there for a while longer until he heard a quiet knock at his door.

"Yeah?" he called.

The door opened to show Charlie, holding a mug. "Hey, you. I didn't want you to sleep too long and not sleep tonight." He raised the cup. "I brought refreshments."

"Come on in." Josh swung his legs over the end of his bed and sat up. Charlie hesitated, then brought the mug to him. "Thanks." Placing the mug on his bedside table, he grabbed Charlie's wrist quickly before he could back away.

"Oh!" Charlie jumped, then whispered, "Josh! Mum's downstairs and the door is open."

Josh wrapped his arms around Charlie's waist and rested his cheek on his stomach. Charlie was tense for a minute before sighing and resting his hands on Josh's hair, stroking gently. Josh relaxed into him, closing his eyes. He wasn't tired anymore; he was content. They stayed like that for a bit, then Josh brushed his face forward so his nose, forehead and chin were touching Charlie's stomach. As he breathed, he took in his essence, moving his nose in circles around his navel.

"Josh?" Charlie whispered again, still stroking his head.

Josh felt the hem of Charlie's t-shirt against his fingertips and slowly ran one hand underneath, feeling the heat of Charlie's bare skin. He skimmed his fingers back and forth across his lower back, all the while rubbing his face against his stomach. Charlie pulled against his hair making Josh lift his face to see him. He could see the question and confusion in Charlie's eyes.

He shook his head as much as Charlie's fingers would allow, then pushed his lips against his navel before removing his hands from under the top and wrapping them around him again. Resting for one minute more, he reluctantly removed his arms, allowing himself the luxury of dragging his fingers down his waist, hips and thighs before letting go. He felt Charlie's fingers caress his face as he pulled his hands away too.

They looked at each other, eyes taking in the details of the other face before Charlie hurriedly bent down and kissed him on the lips, then turned and left, closing the door behind him.

Josh blew out a breath, rubbed his hands over his face and grabbed his tea while it was still warm.

• • • ● ● • ● ● • • •

Dinner was yet again a quiet affair. No one wanted to break the silence with anything other than small talk, even though a discussion was sorely needed. Both Charlie and Josh needed more time to think about things. At least that's what they'd said when their parents had asked to talk to them before dinner.

After eating, Charlie went to his room to get ready for work. Josh was lying on his back on his bed, one knee raised while reading a magazine when Charlie knocked on his doorframe.

"Hey. Do you fancy keeping me company at work tonight? At least for a while. I know you can't stay late because of college tomorrow."

Josh jumped off the bed. "Hell, yeah!" He threw the magazine down and walked to the door.

Charlie laughed. "That eager! Alright, let's go." They descended the stairs. "Bye Mum, Dad. I'm off to work. See you tomorrow."

Charlie looked towards Josh, raising his eyebrows. Josh shook his head, frowning. Charlie tilted his head at him and nodded in their parents' direction.

Josh huffed but said, "I'm heading out with Charlie," then gave him a "happy now?" move and ushered Charlie outside to his car.

Charlie rolled his eyes and unlocked the car. The journey to the bar was quiet with Josh's eyes on the view outside the windows. Parking up, they climbed out and entered the fray.

• • • ● • ● • ● • • •

Watching Charlie was like poetry in motion, and Josh was not at all poetic. He understood the principle, though. Charlie worked hard but efficiently and made sure each customer got his full attention, smiles always available, stern words only needed occasionally but always obeyed. All customers were worried about being banned from Crush. There weren't many people who had been banned, but if you're banned once, you're never let in again. Ever.

Josh watched the play of muscles on Charlie's biceps as he worked the beer pump. He could tell he was staring but couldn't quite help himself. He shrugged his shoulders. People could think what they wanted, for all they know he could be looking past Charlie to something else. He glanced around the bar, noticing the way some of the customers eyed his brother. He narrowed his eyes. He'd never thought about it before, but this was the perfect place for Charlie to find someone else. Someone who was not him.

Charlie was a catch, there was no doubt about it. Yes, he was slim for his age, and he was shorter than some guys, but he had chocolate brown hair colour, which made you want to brush your hands through the thick mass. And those piercing blue eyes. Josh sighed. Dark hair and blue eyes had always been a combination that ruled Josh's choices in the past. He'd only just realised that Charlie was his perfect match in that respect.

Josh tried to turn his mind to something else. He had to; otherwise, he would end up revealing more than necessary. He noticed Analise looking at him, so he smiled and arched his eyebrow in question. She smiled, shaking her head, then looked at Charlie and back at Josh before finishing up with the beer she was pouring. Josh shook his head. He didn't know what that was about.

A couple of hours later, Josh had drunk several beers while watching Charlie work. He was feeling quite tipsy by that point, but everything felt much simpler to him. His parents had lied to him for three years. How could he believe anything they said anymore? And as for Charlie, well, he was his. It was that simple. He nodded his head to himself, lifting his beer to finish it off. Everything made sense tonight. He didn't see what the issues were.

He looked for Charlie to request another beer but found he was already in front of him.

"Hey, you," he said, smiling happily. "I all outta beer. Can you get me 'nother?" he stumbled over his words, even though he was not that drunk.

Charlie smiled at him. "I think you've had enough, Josh. Let's get you into the office. You can sleep it off on the sofa." He turned away to let Analise know what he was doing then came out from behind the bar. "Come on, up you go." Pulling Josh's arm around his shoulders, Charlie manoeuvred Josh through the hallway to the hardly used office.

Once inside, he pushed him down onto the sofa, letting him flop however he landed. Charlie disappeared for a minute, then returned with a glass of water. He knelt next to the sofa, put his arm under Josh's shoulder to raise him while he drank it then laid him down again.

He grabbed Charlie's wrist, pulling him across his chest. "You're gorgeous." He drifted his fingers down Charlie's temple and cheek and across his lips. "Kiss me?" he asked.

Charlie hesitated then leaned up and brushed his lips across Josh's. He threaded his hands through Charlie's hair and deepened the kiss, tasting him with his tongue. Their breaths intermingled as their tongues duelled; the kiss got harder and deeper. Josh grabbed Charlie's hand and moved it to his cock, pressing it against the zipper, allowing him to feel how hard he was. Charlie gasped into Josh's mouth, and his hand curled around the erection without thought, moving up and down slowly. Then Charlie let go, making Josh groan and his hips follow his hand.

"No, not now." Charlie touched his fingers to his kiss-bruised lips. Josh loved knowing he wore his mark. Breathing almost under control, Charlie stood. "Get some sleep. I'll check back on you later." He walked to the door, turning back once it was open. "You'll get a couple of hours." He smiled and closed the door behind him.

Josh groaned and palmed his cock, willing it to go down. Charlie was such a tease. He closed his eyes, breathing deeply to calm down, knowing there was no way he was going to sleep in this state.

The next thing he knew, he was dreaming of Charlie kneeling between his legs, with Josh deep in his throat as he swallowed around him.

"Fuck, Charlie. That's it, suck it deep." He was amazing. Josh looked down at him, watching his cock disappear into his mouth and back out glistening. "Oh, God. I'm not going to last." Charlie gagged once, then placed a hand at the base of his cock, marking how far he could take him, then took him down again. Hollowing his cheeks on the way up, he slipped off and tongued at his slit, licking his head like a lollipop.

"Holy shit!" Josh's hips lifted on their own accord, trying to gain entrance to that mouth again. Charlie smiled, then returned to licking the whole of his shaft, using his hand to pump him. "I'm so close, Charlie, so close." Charlie sucked at the tip, while tonguing his slit, then swallowed him whole. Moving his hand in time with his mouth, he sucked up and down, giving more friction and heat. "Shit, shit!" Josh's voice was loud in the room. On a downward stroke, Charlie allowed himself to swallow around his shaft, gagging and then it was all over. "I'm coming!"

Josh's orgasm made him fly, he was sure of it. He couldn't think at all, just feel the immense pleasure strumming through his body. He was distantly aware of Charlie swallowing his come, before licking him clean. He so wished it had been real, but Charlie was so new to all this and Josh didn't want to bring him deeper into the mess they'd made.

He hovered between consciousness and sleep, before slowly becoming more alert. As he woke properly, he became mindful of a warm body resting against his legs and lower stomach. And then aware of the cold air on his cock.

His eyes slammed open, seeing Charlie smiling up at him from his perch on his abs.

"Hi," he said, blushing. Josh realised what he thought was a dream, was very much real in fact.

"Wow!" That was all he could manage.

He must have slept some before this because his mind felt clearer and he didn't feel drunk. But to have Charlie resting over the top of him like he was, made him sex drunk.

"I thought I was dreaming!" Josh looked over at him in surprise. "Thank you."

Charlie blushed again but smiled. "You're very welcome." Charlie moved off him, then realised he'd left Josh's cock out. He blushed again and moved to put Josh's clothes back to rights.

"It's okay. I'll sort it." Charlie got up and headed off the bathroom. Josh lifted himself to a sitting position, allowing his head to stop swimming before he attempted anything else. Once his mind was centred, he stood, holding on the waist of his jeans to stop them from falling. He tucked himself back in as Charlie came back with another glass of water for him.

"Thought you might need some rehydration," he said, holding out the glass.

"Thanks." He gulped the whole glass in one, resting it on the table once he'd finished. "What time is it?"

"About two-thirty. Once we were all done tidying and cashing up, I sent everyone home, reminding them you were here to help me get home." He blushed again. He really did like those blushes. "I locked up, but we need to get going. I'm tired." And he looked it.

"Okay, let's go." Josh held out his hand and Charlie took it as they walked towards the front of the bar. Exiting, Josh watched him lock everything up, then walked side by side to the car, wishing he could hold Charlie's hand.

On the drive home, he did hold his hand, fingers linked together; like he would if they were in a relationship. *He could wish, couldn't he? Even if it would never happen.*

Letting themselves in the house quietly, they tiptoed up to their bedrooms, Josh following Charlie into his room.

"What-?" He started.

"Shhh." Josh quieted him while he pushed Charlie's door closed, not shutting it completely. "I want to say goodnight." He took him in his arms and kissed him. He kissed him as if he would never get the chance to ever kiss him again. He kissed him as if he was his one and only. He kissed him as if he could never let him go. Ever. All his emotions were wrapped up in the kiss and when they finally broke away, they were gasping for breath, only to jump at a voice.

"What the hell is going on?" Their dad stood in Charlie's doorway, shock and horror on his face.

Charlie and Josh sprang apart. Dread coiled in Josh's stomach, ice freezing the blood in his veins. *Shit!* Josh spared a quick glance at Charlie, seeing him in the same frozen position, before facing Dad again. *What the hell were they going to say?*

Dad looked from Charlie to Josh and back again, before shaking his head, mouth tight. "We are going to sit down in the morning to talk through everything. Both of you go to bed." He didn't quite yell, just got his point across. "Separately!" He moved further into Charlie's room, allowing Josh to pass by him. He saw as his dad looked back at Charlie, forehead creased, pain in his eyes, then followed Josh out, closing the door behind him. Even though he did it quietly, he may as well have slammed it, for the reaction in Josh was the same. He jumped, tears wanting to pour down his cheeks and wrapped his arms around his waist.

He entered his room and laid on the bed. He wished he could see a better outcome than what was playing in his mind now.

9

Josh

Josh slowly descended the stairs the next morning, dreading the upcoming conversation. He'd hardly slept all night, alternating between worrying about what Dad was going to say about him and Charlie, and being angry about their separation. He paused at the bottom step, hearing muted voices in the kitchen. Sighing, he went towards the sound. This was not going to go well.

The voices stopped as he entered the kitchen and made his way to the kettle for a coffee. He needed caffeine for this confrontation. Nobody said anything behind him while he doctored his drink. Taking a breath, he grabbed his mug and turned towards the table. "Morning," he said quietly.

Josh took a sip of his drink and went to sit next to Charlie and opposite their parents. *Wow, this feels like when we were younger.* Resting his mug on the table, he glanced at Charlie, seeing the dark circles under his eyes. He could tell this was killing him. Bracing himself, he glared at his parents. His dad still had the same expression as last night but with added confusion. His mum was wringing her hands together while looking down at them.

"So, we need to get everything out in the open. Your mother and I are ready for you to ask any questions you have." Dad glanced at his wife then back to them.

Josh raised his eyebrows. That was not where he thought they were going to start—he was expecting a tirade about how they were siblings and shouldn't be together because it's wrong. He quickly looked at Charlie again, seeing the surprise reflected in his face.

Although it was a subject he'd thought hard about over the last couple of days, he was thrown off by the topic his dad had chosen. Sitting back in his chair, he thought for a minute.

"Why didn't you tell us?" Charlie's voice was timid and small, cracking slightly. Without thinking, he reached out and covered Charlie's hand with his, then realising what he'd done, glanced at his dad. His dad's jaw tensed as he looked at their joined hands, but he didn't say anything. Looking at his mum garnered him only a small smile from her. Josh's mind whirled. If what he was interpreting was right, Dad hadn't told Mum about what he'd seen last night. Josh frowned at his dad in question. His dad responded with a subtle shake of his head, indicating he had not mentioned anything to her. Yet.

"Well, sweetheart, we didn't tell you to begin with because we didn't want to upset you while you were finishing your exams. I'm so sorry we didn't tell you." Mum's eyes pleaded with them.

"I don't understand how you could have kept it a secret all this time!" Josh's voice was loud. "It's been years since Charlie finished them, and you still didn't say anything."

"I know we didn't. After that, there just seemed to be one thing after another happening, and it never seemed like the right time. I know it's no excuse—"

"It's definitely no excuse. You haven't been in love for years! And you expect us to be okay with this?" Josh shouted, sliding his chair back from the table and flinging his hands around. "How can you pretend?"

"Josh—" Charlie stood, grabbing his arm to try and get him to sit down.

"No, Charlie. He has a right to be angry. You both do," Mum said quietly.

"You're damn right I have a right to be angry."

"Do not speak to your mother like that!" Dad's voice whipped across the kitchen, stopping Josh before he said any more. "If we are to discuss this, you will sit down and listen like the adults you are."

Everyone froze for a moment. Josh stood, hands on hips, breathing deeply. After a moment, he sat back down. Charlie wrapped his arms through Josh's, holding tight. "Sorry." Josh apologised to his mother, looking at her briefly before looking back at the table. "Everything feels like...like it was pretending. I don't know what to do with that," he said softly.

"Oh, Josh!" His mother came around the table and wrapped him in her arms. Her smell reminded him of all the times she had been there for him. So, he let go of everything, hung on to her and sobbed. "I'm so sorry, sweetheart. I'm so sorry." He heard his mum say over and over while rubbing his back.

After a time—he wasn't sure how long—he found himself in a tangle of limbs but feeling lighter than before. He moved, dislodging his mother from around his neck and Charlie from around his waist, realising his dad had hold of his hand on the table. Josh used his free hand to wipe his face of tears and briefly glanced at Charlie. His eyes were suspiciously wet too.

"Sorry about that," he said, clearing this throat. He thanked his mum when she brought over a glass of water for him and one for Charlie. He took hold of the glass, then let go of his dad's hand when he realised his hand was shaking too badly to hold it still. Drinking deeply, he set the empty glass on the table and blew out a breath. He couldn't look at anyone.

"Josh, nothing was ever pretend. Everything you saw, heard and witnessed was real. I love your father very much, and he loves me." They looked at each other, then she looked back at Josh.

"Just because we are not together anymore doesn't mean we love you both any less. You are our sunshines, every single day and will be forever. Your dad and I have not been happy keeping up this pretence, but we have never been unhappy with the situation between ourselves. As I said, we love each other and always will do, but it's time for us to think about the future." Mum smiled gently.

"And what does the future look like?" Charlie asked the question Josh also wanted to know the answer to.

Mum looked at Dad. "We don't know yet, but I will tell you, as of now, there are no significant others involved. So don't concern yourself with having to welcome another person into the family."

"Wow, I don't want to think about that yet." Josh managed a small laugh, rubbing his face again.

"As much as you may expect to see some changes, nothing is really going to change yet. Everything is going to continue as it has been. But this time, we will talk to you about any changes that may come up. And, please, come to us if you have any questions." She reached forward to grab each of their hands, squeezing gently. "We love you. And we're sorry."

"Okay, I can live with that." Charlie glanced at Josh, eyes sad but clearer than when they started the conversation, which was the whole point, he supposed.

"Yeah, okay." He blew out another breath. "I think I need a shower."

"Okay, sweetheart. You head up, and I'll have another coffee ready for you when you come down." Josh got up and headed towards the stairs. "Oh, and Josh?" He looked back at his mother. "Pancakes?" she asked with a twinkle in her eye.

Josh gave a watery smile, ran over to her and gave her a huge hug. He turned around and grabbed his dad for a hug too. Then he ran up the stairs to the shower before the tears got the better of him again.

. . . ● ● . ● . ● . . .

With a towel wrapped around him, he went into his room to get dressed. A knock sounded on his door as he did up his jeans.

"Hold on," he called, grabbing his top and throwing it over his head. Half decent, he opened his door and saw Dad and Charlie. "Hi." He stepped back so they could enter.

Once they were inside, Dad closed the door. "I wanted to let you know I have not said anything to your mother about what I saw last night." Charlie and Josh let out a breath. "But I will be." Dad looked at them both sternly. "I will not keep secrets from her about something like this. I don't know what's going on, but I will tell your mother while you are both out today, and then before dinner, we will sit down and talk things through."

He turned around and walked out the door, leaving the door ajar, making his thoughts visible. Josh looked at Charlie. "Shit."

"Yep." Charlie was staring at the door, deep in thought. He was quiet for a few moments, and Josh let him have space. "We need to stay away from each other, J." He looked at Josh, pain reflected in his eyes. "I know we live in the same house, but...I can't...I can't do this right now. Not on top of everything else. I'm sorry." Charlie left his room, not giving him any chance to respond, shutting his door behind him in finality.

Josh had known it was coming, but it still hurt. He sat on his bed and lost himself in his thoughts. He remembered times when he and Charlie had been messing around when they were younger, then times when they'd been at the same parties before all this had happened. Then he recalled their recent times together. He closed his eyes against the images, but naturally, they became clearer. His heart threatened to beat out of his chest, and his eyes were leaking tears again.

What he felt for Charlie, yes it was wrong, but it felt so real, so right. He didn't know where to go from here. If he talked it through with his parents, things might become clearer. He could hope anyway. But he also knew this was the end of them. There was no way his parents would stand for it.

After a while, he roused himself, looking at his clock. He had already missed his first class of the day but still had several to go, so he got himself ready for college. He hoped he'd be able to concentrate. He also had an apology to make to his tutor. He grabbed his bag and packed it with his books and tools. *You are fine, Josh. You will be fine.* Maybe if he told himself enough times, he would be.

· • • ● ● • ● ● • • ·

After a pancake breakfast, Josh managed to get through his art history class as well as making an extra trip to see the tutor he'd yelled at. He apologised and explained, in brief terms, the situation at home. The tutor was very understanding and let it go, thankfully.

He was on his way to his next class, graphic design, when he heard his name. Turning around, he saw Aiden sauntering towards him, alone for a change. He rolled his eyes and blew out a breath. If he had realised how clingy and annoying the guy would be when they ended their relationship, he would never have started it to begin with.

"What do you want, Aiden?" Josh huffed. Aiden didn't seem to get the picture.

"Is that any way to talk to your boyfriend, Josh?" Aiden stopped in front of him, lifting his cheek to him as if expecting a kiss. When Josh looked at him, Aiden lost the peaceful, friendly face, although kept the tone light. "What no kiss? Shame on you."

"Again, what do you want?" Josh's tone took on a hard edge, but he knew he had to keep it calm because they were at college and other students were milling around.

Aiden huffed. "I want what every other guy wants, sweetie, a man who worships him."

Josh laughed. "Well, that's not me, not now, but good luck." He turned to walk away, halting with Aiden's next words.

"I know all about your little sibling secret." Aiden's voice was very quiet but filled with pure malice, and Josh felt goosebumps rise on his arms and neck. He turned back to him slowly, trying for a neutral expression on his face.

"What are you talking about?" he tried for a confused tone but wasn't sure he managed it.

Aiden smiled, and Josh knew he had failed. "I saw you and Charlie outside college yesterday. Bit cosy, weren't you?" He smirked while walking slowly towards him, eyes never leaving Josh's.

Josh searched Aiden's face for any clue he was telling the truth and saw nothing to show he was lying. "I don't know what you think you saw, but Charlie was just picking me up because of some shit at home." Josh tried to make the small truth believable. If he could play the trouble at home scenario, he might be able to turn this around.

"I didn't believe what I saw, to begin with, so I took a photo. I happened to have my phone in my hand and ready to go. How about that? And did you know it is so much easier to see things in the distance when you zoom in on photos?" Aiden pretended this was news to him, face all innocent. But he got his point across.

Shit. Josh was screwed. Aiden only had that one thing to go on, that he knew of, but he had him by the balls because Josh knew the information could not come out regardless of how benign it might seem. He should have listened to Charlie when he'd said to stop. Yet again, another reason to stay away from his brother. He couldn't be trusted to keep his head around Charlie.

"What do you want?" he asked quietly. He saw triumph and calculation flash in Aiden's eyes.

"I want you." He smiled serenely.

"What do you mean exactly?" Josh wasn't agreeing to anything until he knew what Aiden's plans were, even though he knew he'd probably agree to anything anyway. He couldn't let this come down on Charlie. Him? He could deal with whatever was thrown his way, but he refused to let Charlie come to harm because of rumours that could be proven with photos.

"Parties, get-togethers, being seen together. Exactly like when we were in a relationship."

"Why? Why do you even want me?" Josh couldn't understand why Aiden was so intent on having him when there were other guys he could have, easier and definitely more willing. He was missing something.

"Because you look right. You are the picture-perfect college boyfriend. It makes my life easier to have you on my arm. And if it's not willingly, then I'll make sure it's because you have to be." Aiden had removed all pleasantries from his tone now. It was pure evil cunning.

"So, you want to go back to the way things were before I found out you were cheating? That's all you want?" Josh didn't believe him. It couldn't be that simple.

"Yes. But just remember to turn a blind eye as you have been." Aiden smirked, winking as if sharing a secret. It wasn't much of a secret though, because Aiden must have slept with a large portion of the students already.

Josh was still not convinced this was all Aiden wanted. Josh was going in unaware, but he had his blinders off now, so would be waiting for the other shoe to drop. He also had no choice.

"Fine, but I do have one condition."

"Really? And why should I give you anything?" Aiden raised his eyebrows in question.

"You don't have to, but this is an easy one, and it's not like you'll miss it." Josh was pushing it but had to try.

"I'm listening."

"No intercourse. None whatsoever. Kisses, fine. Hugs, fine. Intercourse, not happening." Josh was firm with his words, but again, in his heart, he knew he'd back down if Aiden insisted.

Aiden looked at him for a moment, narrowing his eyes, then nodded. "Fine, but you make everything look normal. You do everything else the situation demands of you to ensure everyone sees how perfect we are together. Understand?"

Josh nodded slowly. "Yep. When do we start?"

Aiden linked their arms together and began walking towards what he knew was Aiden's class. Escorting him there would make Josh late but he didn't want to push. Aiden chatted animatedly throughout their journey, then turned for a kiss when they arrived.

Even though he felt sick doing it, he pretended to be content like his life depended on it. After seeing Aiden in, he walked slowly to his class, apologising for being late.

Sitting in his seat, Josh grabbed his tools and paper and began the work. His mind was going like a freight train and he didn't know which was way up. He tried, for several minutes, to focus on his design, measuring, drawing, remeasuring until, finally, his mind went clear of everything but his work. This was what he liked about art. There was no specific route he had to follow to create a work of art, and it didn't have to look like what others were expecting it to. He loved the freedom in it, the way he could express himself without restrictions.

It was the reason he had chosen several different subjects. Visual art for him was paints, chalk, pens, where he could express himself in colour. Graphic design allowed him to merge visual art with words. He'd decided to take art history because he was interested in how past artists had managed to become who they wanted to be. And finally, ceramics, because he enjoyed creating something from nothing.

When the bell rang for the end of class, Josh felt more centred than he had been. There wasn't much he could do about Aiden now, and he still had the conversation to get through with his parents when he got home, but he felt calmer.

Josh packed up his things and pushed his chair under the table. Exiting the class, he saw Aiden waiting for him. He lifted his cheek, and Josh kissed it.

"Hey babe, we're heading to the café across the road for lunch. That okay?" Aiden smiled sweetly at him, but he understood the undercurrent to it.

"Sure, no problem. I'm starving." Josh could pretend as well as the next person. He would not let this interfere with Charlie's life. He could put up with Aiden for however long this took. He knew Aiden was heading to Oxford University after college was done, so hopefully, that would be the end of it. Only a month or so to get through. It was possible.

The group entered the café and grabbed the booth next to the window. Aiden slid in, pulling Josh in tight next to him, then raising Josh's arm over his head, he placed it firmly around his waist. Josh looked at him with raised eyebrows.

Aiden smiled. "I want you close, babe."

"I can see that." Josh wanted to move away but refrained. Instead, he focused on the menu, hoping he could eat. Even though he was starving, he didn't know how much he could stomach.

He heard the group talking around him but didn't pay attention to their words. When the waitress came to take their order, he chose a club sandwich and coffee. Aiden pulled a face. He was vegetarian and had been trying for months to get Josh to change his diet, but he refused. Before though, he would have refrained from eating it when he was with Aiden, but he didn't care today. Now he would have to put up with it.

His attention was taken by Kent and Carla entering the café. He saw Kent notice him and nodded in greeting. Kent's eyes went wide when he saw who was sat with Josh, understandably, but only jerked his head asking Josh to come over.

"Hey. I'm going over to see Kent and Carla for a minute. I'll be back in a few." Josh shifted across the seat to get up. Aiden caught his hand, squeezing it in warning.

"Okay, sweetie, see you in a min." Josh caught the look he gave him and nodded in acceptance. He knew he would not be saying anything to Kent about their little agreement. Walking over to them, Josh joined them at the counter, sitting next to Kent.

"Hey, how're things?" He tried to keep things casual but knew Kent would ask.

"Fine. What's going on with you though? Last time I saw you two, you were at each other throats and you refused to be with him ever again!" Kent looked briefly at the booth where Aiden was laughing at something someone had said.

He smirked a little and shrugged, trying to come off unbothered. "Better the devil you know, sometimes, eh?" He laughed a little, hoping Kent would drop it.

Kent searched his face for a minute, then nodded slowly. "Sure. How's Charlie? Not seen him at any parties recently."

Josh's heart began to gallop at hearing Charlie's name. He cleared his throat before talking. "He's good. Covering staff holidays at the bar this week so he's not been able to get out."

"He'll be running that bar before he knows it at this rate." Kent's eyes were bright with laughter.

Josh joined him. "That's the plan."

Kent looked over at the table again. "You best get back to Aiden. I'm getting death looks from him now." He glanced at Josh, then the menu which had been placed in front of him.

"Alright, man. I'll see you soon. Bye, Carla."

"Bye, Josh." Carla had kept quiet during the conversation. Josh knew she didn't like Aiden but would never voice anything against him either.

"Josh?" Kent's voice stopped him from leaving. Josh looked at him in question. "Be careful, okay. Just...be careful." Kent looked uncertain, which at any other time Josh would push for an explanation for, but now he needed Kent to let it go. Josh nodded but didn't say anything.

Sitting back at the table, Josh began to eat his lunch. Before he could get very far, Aiden interrupted him.

"Babe, we're okay to go to a party tonight, aren't we? Colin's parents are out of town and have actually bought beer for us!" Aiden laughed. "God help them with the clean-up."

"Sorry, I can't make it tonight. Family dinner."

Aiden narrowed his gaze at Josh, lips pursing. He knew he would hear about it later but, regardless of whether Aiden thought it was an excuse, he couldn't miss this dinner. Aiden didn't know his and Charlie's secret was out at home, and Josh was not going to enlighten him. He might turn it around on his parents too, bringing them into the gutter. Josh would not allow it.

Lunch continued to be a long affair until he made noises about being late for the next class. Aiden let him go with a kiss meant to prove a point. *Point received, Aiden.*

Practically running to ceramics, he managed to get there just in time and lost himself in the world of clay.

10

Charlie

Charlie had spent some of the day wandering around the shops. After leaving Josh's room that morning, he'd been broken. He hadn't wanted to end things as he did, but he had seen no other option. There was no way his heart could continue on the path they had been going down. It might already be too late, but he had to close it off.

He wandered around some of his favourite clothes and trinket shops, only distantly aware of what he was looking at. Nothing took his fancy though, so he decided to go for a drink. Spying a small coffee bar, he made his way over. He took a seat at the counter and placed his order. It was early but he needed something to eat, so ordered a small variety platter to nibble at.

"Charlie!" He turned when he heard his name, then smiled wide and jumped off the stool.

"Hey! What are you doing here? Nice to see you out of the bar." He gave Tom a hug, feeling the hesitancy in Tom's return, so squeezed him gently and whispered, "It's okay Tom, don't worry. I don't mind." He pulled back and smiled at him, seeing the relief on Tom's face.

"I'm here for a spot of lunch before Ginny meets me. Do you want to join me?" Tom made the offer sincerely.

"No, no. I'm fine here. You go, have fun." Charlie waved him off. He loved how happy Ginny had looked when he'd last seen her and if the stars in Tom's eyes were any indication, the feeling was mutual. She would want for nothing ever again.

Returning from his thoughts to the conversation, he heard Tom talking to him. "—not a problem. You're welcome to join me," Tom said, nodding.

"No, honestly, I'm not great company today. So, shoo, go." Charlie made a go away motion with his hands and went to sit down.

"Nope, not happening." Tom grabbed Charlie's wrist and dragged him to the table, after allowing Charlie to collect his things from the counter.

"You're supposed to be meeting Ginny! You don't need me here with you," Charlie grumbled after being pushed onto a chair.

"I know I don't. But you're my friend, and I'm sure Ginny would agree. You're eating with me." Tom smiled. "And anyway, I want to help cheer you up. I can do that while I wait for Ginny. How are you?" Charlie looked down at the table.

"I'm—" Charlie began.

"If you tell me you're fine, I'll smack your backside!"

Charlie's eyes widened at that, and he spluttered a laugh before replying with, "I never knew you were interested in that?" he asked with an eyebrow raise. "Ginny has a lot to tell me!" Charlie paused, then laughed when Tom blushed bright red.

"Don't change the subject!" Tom sobered a moment. "I hope you don't mind, but Ginny told me about the situation with Jimmy. She needed someone to talk to. I saw her worrying about something and told her she needed to tell me. I'm sorry if that wasn't what you wanted her to do."

Charlie stayed silent for a moment, collecting his thoughts. He couldn't tell him about Josh, for obvious reasons, so he explained about the conversation that morning with his parents and Josh's reaction. He also filled him in about what happened when he went to pick Josh up after leaving Ginny the other day.

"How are you feeling about it all?" asked Tom. He had ordered a spicy chicken wrap when the waitress had appeared and was neatly tucking into it. If Charlie had chosen that, it would be all over his shirt by now.

Focusing on his question, Charlie answered, "I'm not sure in all honesty. I can understand why they thought they had to keep it secret during my exams but not why it took them so long after. Three years! It's mind-boggling. I keep trying to think back and see what would have stopped them from telling us, but I can't think of anything." He shook his head. "Anyway, we know now, and they've said they are not planning on making any rash changes any time soon." Charlie picked at his food. "I don't think it's properly sunk in yet."

Tom put his food down and reached over to pat his hand. "Give it time. You may need to speak with them again several times before it will all make sense." He gave him a small smile. "Well, Ginny and I are heading to the cinema after this, and I think you should join us. We're seeing the new action flick. It will have loads of bloody bodies and carnage and violence and who knows what else!" Tom laughed. "That will be sure to take your mind off things."

"Look, Tom, thanks for inviting me to lunch. And to the cinema. But I will be okay. I don't like intruding on your plans. I'll head home and catch up on some much-needed sleep." Charlie doubted it would happen, but he could at least try.

"No, if you need to sleep that badly, you can do it in the theatre!" Tom replied. "Oh, one question, have you heard anything from Jimmy?"

Charlie looked at Tom. "I've heard nothing. I've not seen him nor heard anything from him at all. I don't know whether to be happy or worried about it." Charlie had to admit to himself he was a little worried. It was so unlike Jimmy to let a slight go unopposed.

"Mmm, I'm not sure if I like that," Tom said, echoing his own thoughts. "I don't know Jimmy personally, only what gossip I've heard, but from what Ginny has told me it's out of character." Tom finished his wrap and pushed his plate to the side. "Anyway, let's pay up and head out." Tom waved at the waitress to get the bill. He paid for Charlie's lunch as well, ignoring his protests.

"You're my friend and my best worker, it's the least I can do," Tom said, "and if you tell Rob or Analise I said that I will deny all knowledge." He effected a put-upon air, making Charlie laugh. "Which also reminds me, I'm going to be starting on the plans for sorting out the garden area of the bar. You know as well as I do that it doesn't get used very much with the weather as it is, so the owner is thinking of making it a sheltered area. It has such a stunning view of the river; the owner wants to try and capitalise on it." Tom indicated out the window and Charlie saw Ginny waving at them from across the road. They walked outside and waited for her to cross. "So, just in case you see any men walking around and asking questions."

Ginny reached for Tom when she arrived and gave him a sweet kiss, then followed up with a more platonic one for Charlie. "Hey, Charlie, fancy seeing you here."

"Hey, Gin."

"I've invited him to join us at the cinema, but he's refusing." Tom threw Charlie under the Ginny bandwagon. Charlie threw a daggered look at him, but Tom just smiled.

"Oh, you've got to come with us. You'll enjoy it. Please, Charlie?" She clasped her hands in front of her, begging him.

"Fine, fine! I'll come along and be the third wheel and ruin your date." Charlie huffed, good-naturedly.

"You won't be ruining anything." Ginny hooked her arm around Tom's waist. "We can still have a date with you there."

Charlie noticed a couple of stares and shakes of the head of people from behind Tom and Ginny. The age gap didn't seem to make any difference in how they treated each other. Everyone had different opinions, but so long as the people involved were happy, what did it matter?

Charlie paused at that. The thought centred him a little, but he shook it off realising it was a futile hope. Josh and he were siblings. That was a whole other ballgame to an age gap.

The walk to the cinema didn't take long. Fifteen minutes later, they were at the kiosk buying tickets, drinks and snacks. Charlie stopped when he saw Ginny looking behind him, brows drawn down. "What's the matter, Gin?" Charlie went to turn around, but she caught his arm.

"I didn't know Jimmy knew Aiden," she said quietly, still watching behind him discreetly.

Charlie was unsure where this conversation was going, so answered, "It's not impossible for them to know each other, but I've never seen them together. They certainly don't follow the same social circles. Why?" Charlie was curious why this had caught her eye. He went to turn around, but again, she stopped him. Instinct told him to stay where he was.

"I don't like this, Charlie. They should not be meeting together, not alone anyway. You always told me Aiden was never without his followers. Well, there's no one there with him now." Ginny quickly looked Charlie in the eyes, smiling. "They're leaving." She turned away to pick up her drink from the counter. After checking behind her to make sure they *had* left, Ginny turned back to him. "I didn't see exactly what was going on, but there was a lot of hand movements, then Aiden showed Jimmy his phone. After, Aiden gave Jimmy some paper. That was right before they left."

Charlie thought for a moment but couldn't think of a reason why that would have happened. Aiden and Jimmy were not in the same circles and, knowing Jimmy's reputation, Charlie was concerned about this turn of events. He knew Josh had ended his relationship with Aiden because he was a cheating shit, but there was very little reason for Aiden to go to Jimmy. Charlie also couldn't think of a reason why Jimmy would need Aiden.

Charlie went into the film showing unnerved by it all.

• • • • ● • ● ● • • •

Charlie, Ginny and Tom came out of the cinema laughing. Charlie had a great time with them both and was glad they had pressed for him to join them. He had forgotten about seeing Aiden and Jimmy until they had come to a stop outside the cinema. Just as they were about to part ways, Charlie saw Jimmy across the street, looking at his phone while resting back against the building opposite. A shiver went down Charlie's spine. He twisted around so his back was to the road.

"Hey, Gin!" Charlie waved her and Tom over. Indicating over his shoulder, he looked at Tom. "Is it me or is it weird that Jimmy is here again? I feel like he's keeping an eye on me. It's starting to freak me out. Especially as I've only just told you he hadn't retaliated."

Tom looked over Charlie's shoulder towards Jimmy without making it too obvious. "He's on his phone, although it looks like he's pointing it this way. He could be taking photos. I wonder what is going on?" Tom looked deep in thought, and Ginny looked confused, just like Charlie.

"I think maybe we should get going. I don't like the idea of you walking back alone, Charlie, so we'll come with you." Tom had a frown on his face as he looked towards Jimmy again. "He's leaving now, but we can't be too careful."

Charlie looked around and saw Jimmy smirk at him, then turn and walk in the opposite direction. He blew out a breath. "I hate to say it, but I made a mistake with him. A huge one."

"Yeah, you did. I would recommend making sure someone is with you when you're walking at night," Tom said. He held up his hand, halting Charlie's protest. "I know you would be okay, but if not for your sake then think of your family and friends. They would prefer you safe until we figure out what's going on."

Ginny nodded in agreement. "I hate the idea that Jimmy is cooking up something. It seemed like he was taking a photo, or maybe even a video. But for what end, I don't know."

Charlie shook his head. "I've no idea either. Well, there's nothing we can do about it now. Come on, let's go."

They started walking back towards the main street to where Charlie's car was parked. After exchanging hugs in goodbye, Charlie got in his car and drove home. He mulled everything over in his mind. He had no idea what Jimmy was doing, or Aiden, but his instincts were telling him whatever it was, it was not good. As much as he hated the idea of inconveniencing someone, he was going to take Tom's advice and make sure he had an escort at night. Starting that night. He would ask Josh at dinner if he could be there to pick him up after his shift tonight; his dad wouldn't like the idea but needs must. He needed to find an excuse though, so he didn't have to tell his parents why he needed the escort.

11

Josh

J osh trudged slowly towards the coffee shop to grab a take-away cup for his walk home. He thought the fresh air would help clear his mind before the confrontation that was awaiting him. That was another reason why he decided to walk; it would delay it a little. He hated the idea of disappointing his mum, but Dad was right when he said they needed to get it out in the open. Maybe Mum could help him sort out his head.

Paying for his drink, he added milk at the counter, then attached the lid and started his journey. He didn't know how Mum was going to react. His imagination was running wild, seeing images of her spitting in his face, throwing things and telling him she was wrong and didn't love him anymore. Maybe he should have gone home quicker to get it over with, but then he'd lose it all.

And he deserved it, didn't he? Hadn't he taken advantage of Charlie when he was upset? Hadn't he initiated most of their indiscretions? He was a horrible person. Maybe he should just not return. He stopped in the middle of the path, thinking that thought through to the end. If he did that, Charlie would be free of him, and his parents wouldn't have to deal with the possible repercussions of what they'd done. But then he knew they would worry about him until they knew where he was.

He started moving again, a little quicker this time. He would return, face the discussion, then tell them he was going to find a place of his own. It would allow Charlie the relief of not seeing him anymore. He could live his life, without the reminder of what Josh had done.

He arrived home shortly before three-thirty, knowing they needed to get the conversation done, then Charlie could go to work, and he'd start searching for new places to live. Dropping his bag on the stairs, he made his way to the kitchen. That seemed to be the place where the difficult discussions took place lately. Everyone was sitting in the same seats as this morning, so he shrugged off his coat and hooked it on the back of the chair.

Dad started talking, "I have explained to your mother what I witnessed last night. We are both a little shocked about it and a lot confused but…" His dad paused and seemed to be struggling with his words.

"…But we have one more thing we need to speak with you about," his mum finished. Mum and Dad looked at each other, then Dad reached over and grabbed Mum's hand. "When we talked this morning, we felt really bad for keeping our separation from you." His mum kept her eyes on the table. "But we do have to tell you something else, and I don't really know how you will react."

Josh looked at Charlie, seeing worry creasing his face. He looked back at his parents. "Just tell us. It can't be half as bad as what we are probably thinking right now."

They were silent a beat longer, then Dad dropped a bomb, "Charlie, you're adopted."

Josh stared at his parents, frozen in shock. He turned towards Charlie when a noise sounded. He was sitting there staring at their parents, tears rolling down his cheeks, hands gripped together in his lap. Josh swung his legs around the chair, so he was sitting sideways and rested his hand over Charlie's. He moved his other hand to grip the back of Charlie's neck, trying to ground him.

"Charlie, we are so sorry we didn't tell you. God, it feels like all we've done is kept secrets from you two. I'm sorry, sweetheart. Please don't think this changes anything. You were ours from the minute they placed you in our arms at two hours old." Mum rested her hands on the table as if to reach forward but stopped herself. "Your Dad and I didn't think we could have children. We had tried for many, many years. Eventually, we went to the doctors for tests and were told it was highly unlikely we would be able to conceive because of our ages. We decided to go through the adoption process, and we were given such a precious gift in you." Mum shook her head and smiled. "Then two months later, we found out I was pregnant. Yet another miracle, especially as I was forty-one."

"Charlie, I know this seems like a lot to take in, but you see why we needed to tell you. We don't understand what is going on with you and Josh, and we do need to talk about it, but we couldn't keep it a secret any longer." Dad was firm with his words, but it seemed to anger Charlie.

Josh let go of Charlie as he leant forward, staring at their parents. "You made me think I was disgusting because I had feelings for my brother! You made me second guess everything I've been brought up to think! You're damn right you couldn't keep it a secret! You should have told me years ago! Why wouldn't you say something like that? Why keep it a secret? Yet another bloody secret!" Charlie was in full tirade mode now. It didn't happen very often, but when it did, it took a lot to calm him. He stood, making his chair scrape back and thrust his hands into his hair. "I don't know what to do with this right now!" Charlie moved away from the table.

"Charlie, wait! Let's talk this through. Let us help you to understand!" Mum got up, reaching as if to hug Charlie, but he flinched away from her. Mum crumpled back onto her seat, crying and watching Charlie leave the room. Dad enveloped Mum in a hug and looked at Josh.

"Well, that was not what I was expecting," Josh said with a sigh. "I'll go talk to him."

"Wait." Dad stopped him before he could stand. "Leave him for a few minutes and tell us what's going on with you two."

"I think this is a conversation Charlie needs to be a part of, don't you?" Josh asked, raising his eyebrows.

"And he will be, but I want to know your take on this." Dad's words were insistent, but Josh wasn't budging.

"No, I'm not talking about this without Charlie here. He deserves to know what is being said about this situation. If we talk about him behind his back, he'll retreat further. I know him. And so do you." Josh stared at his father, before standing and leaving the room.

Walking slowly up the stairs, Josh tried to collect his thoughts before he got to Charlie. He wasn't sure there was anything he could say that would make this easier for him. Knocking on Charlie's door, he heard him mumble, "Come in."

Josh let himself in, seeing Charlie sat on his bed in the far corner of the room, resting against the window, knees bent. He looked so small in that position. "Hey." Josh didn't know what else to say, so he climbed onto the bed and sat next to Charlie.

They sat in silence for a few minutes until Charlie turned his face towards Josh. "I don't know whether to be grateful our situation is not as fucked up as we had originally believed or pissed off *my* situation is fucked up." Charlie laughed half-heartedly. He took a breath and shook his head. "I can't believe I'm adopted," he whispered, brokenly.

Josh turned and folded Charlie in his arms as the dam broke. It was his turn to provide comfort. Charlie cried until his breathing was sounding as hoarse as his voice, and Josh held him through it all, even when it slowed a little. His heart was breaking for Charlie, but in the same breath, was singing in joy. In the back of his head, he was happy because it meant what had happened between them wasn't wrong. Well, at least not as wrong as they thought. After having that thought, he chastised himself because it should be the last thing on his mind when Charlie was going through it all.

Charlie pulled away a little, sniffling as he moved. He used the heel of his hand to wipe his face dry. Josh kept his arm around him but loosened so Charlie could move away if he wanted to. Josh hoped he didn't though. After another sniff, Charlie looked over at Josh then leaned over and kissed him. Just a brief peck of his lips but it was a kiss, nonetheless. When Charlie moved back, Josh cupped his cheek, brushing his thumb over Charlie's cheekbone.

"I suppose we don't need to worry as much about it now, do we?" Charlie said quietly.

"Well, not officially. But I have a feeling some people will still see it as a bad thing." Charlie's face fell, and Josh realised Charlie had misunderstood. He quickly continued. "Not that I do. I didn't want to say this out loud but, in some ways, I'm glad this has happened. Not because of it hurting you, but because it's given us some freedom."

Charlie searched Josh's face for something then smiled and nodded. "I know. It's going to take some getting used to."

Josh's heart soared in hope, but he refrained from pinning Charlie down for a more in-depth explanation. "How are you feeling?"

"I don't really know to be honest. The main things going around my head are the lies which seem to be piling up and the fact I'm apparently not as disgusting as I thought I was." Charlie said it with such conviction it shocked Josh. Yes, okay, they were brought up as siblings, but Josh would never have said they were disgusting. He supposed it would be difficult for a lot of people to get their heads around, though.

"Even when it was wrong, it never felt that way to me, Charlie. I didn't want to admit it, but it feels more. In here." Josh tapped his chest. "I don't understand it, but it feels different from when I knew you as my brother. I can't explain it."

Charlie rested his head against Josh again and sighed. "I know what you mean. I don't understand it either. I would never have admitted this before, but I have dreamt about you for a long time—much longer than I should have, and I tried to keep a distance."

They stayed in companionable silence for a while before Josh's stomach rumbled. Charlie cracked up. "Maybe we should go and finish the discussion with Mum and Dad so we can get you fed." Charlie poked a finger at Josh's abs. "You'll scare little children with that noise."

Josh caught Charlie's finger and pulled him, so he was laid half over him. He gently kissed him before pulling back. "There. That will tide us over."

They both got up and traipsed downstairs to the scent of cooking. Entering the kitchen first, Josh saw Mum at the oven and, by the smell, she was cooking stir fry. Mum looked up, saw them both and smiled a little. "I hope you're hungry."

Charlie burst out laughing, causing Mum to jump and stare. "Ha, ha, very funny Charlie." Josh rolled his eyes and walked to the drawer to get the cutlery. Charlie was still chuckling when Josh brought them to the table. In a way, it might be cathartic for Charlie to laugh, allowing him to relax a little and try to get back some semblance of peace.

"Did I miss the joke?" Dad asked as he came through the door.

"Charlie thinks he's a comedian," Josh replied, sitting down.

"No, I don't. You're the one who is likely to scare children." Charlie chuckled again. "Josh's stomach rumbled so loud I'm surprised you didn't hear it." Josh could see Charlie was struggling a little to keep the jovial sound to his voice, but he was trying. And so were his parents. They laughed along with him.

They kept the conversation light while Mum was dishing up the food, asking Josh about college and Charlie about his work.

"Oh, that reminds me. J, I was going to ask if you wanted to nip in before I finish tonight so I could show you how to close the bar up?" Charlie looked at him with an intensity that pricked Josh's instincts.

"Sure, that's a good idea." Josh didn't know what the underlying tension was about, but he kept his tone neutral. Glancing at his dad, he saw him frown a little, looking between the two of them, but he didn't say anything.

During dinner, they talked about general topics: things they'd heard on the news, gossip from family and friends. Josh could see the clock ticking towards five and knew Charlie had to get ready and drive to work soon, so he brought the conversation around to where it needed to go.

He cleared his throat. "We don't really know what's going on between us, in all honesty." Josh couldn't quite look at them yet. "We knew we weren't supposed to be together, but it just kept happening. I know it seems like an excuse; I can't explain it any other way." Josh chanced a look at his parents. He saw confusion and a little fear in their eyes, but he gave them credit, they didn't scream or yell or shout at them. That was a bonus in his books.

"So, what I saw was not the first time something had happened?" his dad asked.

Josh shook his head, clearing his throat again.

"I don't want all the details, but how far has it gone?" his mum asked, her face showing no discomfort at the personal question. But then again, she had raised two boys and talked through puberty and sex with them. They should all be over the embarrassment aspect now.

Charlie coughed a little, clearly a little more uncomfortable than Josh was. "Not that far," he said quietly.

Mum nodded. "Well, we can't tell you what to do. It's your choice at the end of the day. You have to live with any consequences." She took a breath. "But we do have to tell you what those consequences may be. You need to understand everything, from our point of view as well as other people's. We love you both. If you want to try for a relationship together, then we will support you, which I'm sure will surprise you, but please think carefully."

"Outside of this house, people will not take kindly to your relationship," Dad began. "People will not understand how you can feel what you say you do towards a sibling, regardless of the fact you are not blood-related. Some people will not see that, or they will not care. All they will see are two brothers in a sexual relationship."

"We know it's not conventional, and we've not even talked properly about it yet," Josh stated. "We know there is something, but we still need to discuss what we want and the parameters of that."

Charlie jumped in, "We're not going to rush into anything."

"Good. As I said, we will support you whatever you decide. You need to be prepared for uncomfortable situations," Mum said.

"And for losing family and friends." Dad looked at them both. "You may lose some friends who you thought would stick with you through everything. Then again, they may surprise you and not be bothered. You may end up having words shouted at you in the street, graffiti on your cars, and things like that. I'm not trying to get you to change your minds. I want you prepared."

Josh glanced at Charlie, and they both nodded. "We understand. As soon as we have decided, we will let you know what's going on."

"Okay, then. Off to work with you," Mum said, waving her hands at Charlie. "I'll have your lunch ready by the time you leave." She got up and started bustling around the kitchen.

Josh looked at his dad. "Thanks." His dad nodded.

12

Charlie

"Hey, Charlie."

"Oh, hi, Johnson. How're things?" Charlie wiped the bar in front of the man, then turned to get his regular order.

"Good, thanks. Work is crazy busy as always. I knew I'd be busy as a lawyer, but this even exceeds my expectations." Johnson laughed, shaking his head. "At least I can come here to wind down. Although it might be different when you're gone."

His words didn't register properly with Charlie until he'd almost filled the pint. When they did, he looked at Johnson in confusion. "When I'm gone?" Charlie laughed. "Why, where am I going?" He finished the pint and set it in front of Johnson, leaning on the bar after checking no one needed him.

"I heard you were leaving for another bar. Someone said you were biding your time until the position became available. I was surprised, to be honest, because I thought you were a lifer." Johnson took a big gulp.

Charlie was shocked. "Where did you hear that? I'm not going anywhere unless I get fired unless someone knows something I don't."

"I heard it when I was in Pop's earlier. Some guys your age were talking about you and your plans." Johnson shook his head.

"I may have been mistaken though, but I'm sure that was what they were saying. Anyway, I'm glad it's not true. You'd be missed. You're a part of this bar as much as the counter we're resting on." Johnson smiled, his eyes flicking towards the door. "Ah, here's my date. Thanks for the beer, Charlie. Can you open a tab as normal, please?"

Charlie waved him away. "Of course. Have fun." Johnson left to greet his date, a guy who looked to be ten years his junior, but they looked happy. Charlie knew Johnson had not had much luck in the romance department because of the long hours he had to work. He spent all his time between work, the bar and his home.

Pushing the conversation to the back of his mind, he carried on with work after checking the time. Tom should be there in half an hour. He normally came in for a close to make sure none of them was alone, but he wasn't able to that night—he had a proper date with Ginny. That was why Charlie had asked Josh to come to the bar later.

When Tom arrived, he went straight to the office with barely a nod at Charlie. He frowned. Tom always stopped at the bar to chat for a few minutes, even if it was just to get an update. On his heels was Analise. She came rushing in, not even taking her bag to the office as she usually did. She came straight around the bar and grabbed his arm.

"What's going on?" Charlie asked as he almost stumbled into her.

"What's going on! I should ask you the same question! Why are you leaving the bar? I thought you wanted the manager position when Tom finished?" Analise threw the words at him, anger blazing in her eyes. "Tom is really upset. He thinks you're leaving because you're not getting the manager position quick enough. What the hell is going on?"

Charlie reeled back. This was the second time this topic had come up tonight; something wasn't sitting right. "Nothing's going on! Where did you hear this? Johnson said something similar earlier, but you know me, Analise. You know I wouldn't do this to Tom. Why are you even questioning it?" Charlie was annoyed Analise—and Tom—seemed to think so little of him, especially having known him for as long as they had.

"I thought I did, but I've heard several people say the same thing." Analise looked a little hurt. "I thought you'd talk to me about it."

"Analise, I am not planning on leaving. Who's been saying I am?" Charlie was getting frustrated now. It seemed someone was trying to make his life difficult...then his mind connected the dots. "Jimmy," he said in anger. "Analise, can you take over for a few minutes. I need to go and see Tom." Charlie didn't wait for her answer, just edged around her and went to the office. He entered without knocking and found Tom sat at the desk with his head in his hands. He distantly noted that the blinds were closed, unusual for the daytime.

"Tom?" Charlie asked quietly.

Tom looked up, sadness in his eyes. "Why didn't you tell me you were fed up of waiting, Charlie?"

"Tom, please listen. I don't know exactly what you've heard, but I'm not leaving unless you fire me. Remember we saw Jimmy earlier?" He waited for Tom's nod. "Well, I think he's spreading the rumours. Johnson asked me about it earlier as well, and then Analise. I promise I'm not leaving, and I'm not fed up. This bar is where I want to be. Please believe me." Charlie begged Tom to listen to him and not the gossip.

Tom looked at him for a minute, then nodded his head. "I must admit I was shocked when I heard it. I'm sorry. I jumped to the wrong conclusion. I should have known you better than that. It's always been in the back of my mind you should take over this bar sooner rather than later, but you keep putting it off saying you're not ready." Tom leaned back in his chair, relief visible on his face. "You may be on to something with Jimmy. This sounds like something he might do, and come to think about it, I've been getting phone calls for a couple of weeks now from someone trying to get me to take him on. Travis somebody. He calls at least once a day. It's getting tiresome."

Charlie blew out a breath, thankful Tom wasn't upset. "Why don't you interview him, we could do with an extra bartender to cover holidays."

"I would, but the only position he wanted was the manager position." Tom looked at Charlie and winked. "That position is filled, currently and for the foreseeable future."

"Wow, it seems presumptuous to insist on the manager's position only. Seems like you're right about this Travis guy. Steer well clear." Charlie laughed. "You have to applaud his determination and drive though. I wouldn't have the balls to do that."

"I do to a certain degree, but tenacity only goes so far. You have to have decency to go with it." Tom sat a little straighter. "Anyway, get back out there. Analise is probably overrun by now. I'll be out in a minute."

Charlie nodded and strode back to the bar, feeling more at ease; now he just had to explain things to Analise. She eyed him as he came back but didn't say anything until she'd finished with her current customer.

"I promise you, Analise, I'm not leaving. We think Jimmy is spreading rumours because he didn't get what he wanted from me the other night."

"You were with Jimmy?" Analise said, shock coating her voice.

Charlie realised he hadn't spoken to Analise properly for a few days, so during the rest of the shift, he explained that his date had been with Jimmy. She was speechless but once he'd explained about seeing Jimmy outside the cinema earlier, she said the rumours made sense to be coming from him.

Tom left about nine, and Analise when her shift finished at twelve. Charlie was left tending the bar while the stragglers finished their evening. Only five customers were remaining, and they were sat chatting in two groups, nursing the drinks they'd ordered a while ago. Charlie cleaned up behind the bar, making sure the bottles were closed, lemon and lime were put in the fridge and glasses were put in the dishwasher. He cleaned down the counter and the pumps, then emptied the bins and placed the bags by the back door; he'd put them outside when Josh got there.

He turned and saw the last of the customers leave with a wave. He blew out a breath. Twelve forty-five according to his watch. It would be about an hour before Josh turned up. Now everyone had left, he could lift the chairs and mop the floor. He went over to the old-style jukebox to put some music on while he finished up.

He went through the room, lifting the chairs onto the tables, swaying his hips to the music and singing along with some of the words. He was not a singer in any way, but he loved listening to music. He went into the cleaning cupboard in the back hallway to get the mop and bucket, then wheeled it back through to the bar area.

Charlie came to an abrupt halt when he realised someone was in the bar. He frowned. *How had they got in? I locked the door*, he thought, then frowned harder, *or did I?* Walking further into the bar, he froze when he saw Jimmy sitting at the counter.

"How did you get in?" Charlie asked him, trying to hide how uncomfortable he was in Jimmy's presence.

"You really should lock the door behind you," Jimmy drawled, twirling a beer mat between his fingers. He sat on a stool, resting one arm on the counter and one in his jeans pocket. He was staring at Charlie with a small smile on his face.

"I did lock it," Charlie countered. At least he thought he had.

"Well then maybe you need to start double-checking because it was definitely unlocked." Jimmy smirked. "It's worked in my favour tonight. I needed to have a chat with you without any distractions."

"What about?" Charlie said, still frozen; he wasn't planning on moving any time soon.

Jimmy stood from the stool, throwing the beer mat back onto the counter and sauntered around the room. He didn't walk directly to Charlie but in a wide circle, reminding him of a vulture. He turned his head with Jimmy's movements, always making sure to keep Jimmy in his eye line.

"Well, I have an acquaintance who would like to see his brother in prime position at this bar. So, it means you need to step down." Jimmy paused his walk to make eye contact with Charlie.

"It *was* you spreading the rumours." Charlie was impressed by Jimmy's plan, but also a little scared.

"Of course, but not just me. My acquaintance has a specific interest in not only seeing his brother here but keeping a relationship going with someone close to him."

"So, you just want me to quit?" Charlie wanted to make sure he knew what Jimmy was asking.

"Yes. By doing that, his brother can take your position and take over from Tom sooner rather than later. And by doing *that*, he also gets something to hold over someone else." Jimmy feigned boredom. "I'm not interested in that part of the plan, just the bit involving you." He started towards Charlie again, directly this time. "I've come to get what I'm owed, Charlie."

Charlie froze in place. He wouldn't have been able to move if his life depended on it. And it just might.

Jimmy stood directly in front of Charlie and reached a fingertip to his cheek, making Charlie flinch. Jimmy chuckled as he drew his finger down Charlie's jawline. Then he grabbed Charlie around the neck and shoved him back towards the hallway. He would have fallen had Jimmy not had such a good hold on his neck. As it was, he choked, dropping the mop to the floor. Charlie was scared, really scared. He'd thought he knew the type of man Jimmy was but realised now unless he could get away, this would end badly.

Jimmy practically threw Charlie through the office door, making him flail and land on the floor. He scrambled backwards until he felt the sofa behind him.

"Jimmy, wait," Charlie said, holding his hand out, trying to make him see reason but looking into his eyes, he knew there was no hope.

Jimmy grabbed Charlie by his hair and lifted him onto the sofa, turning him so he fell face first. Charlie tried to get his hands beneath him to push himself up, but Jimmy's weight followed him down, stopping him from moving and trapping his hands under his chest. Jimmy slid his hands towards the front of Charlie's trousers, grabbing the button and undoing it forcefully. Charlie was helpless, he couldn't move at all, could hardly breathe.

His trousers were yanked down his legs as far as they could go and some of the weight moved off him briefly. He felt a hand press hard on his upper back as he heard another zipper being undone. Charlie could breathe better now, but he began to panic. He couldn't allow Jimmy to do this, but he didn't know how to get away. He was panting so heavily his vision started to spot. Jimmy was talking, but he couldn't understand the words.

He felt warm skin moving against his ass, and he bucked. He heard Jimmy chuckle as if from miles away. The sensation of skin sliding across his abruptly stopped, though he knew Jimmy was still pressed tight.

"Fuck! You're so lucky this time, Charlie. Next time, I'll make sure we won't be disturbed. Let's hope Aiden doesn't get tired of waiting," Jimmy whispered angrily in his ear, spit drifting down Charlie's cheek. At that, the weight was gone, and Charlie felt cool air on his ass and legs. He heard a click, footsteps, then the bang of the back door being shut.

"Charlie! Are you in here?" Distantly, he heard Josh's voice coming from the hallway. There was silence, then, "Fucking hell, Charlie, what happened?" He felt hands grab his trousers and pull them up. Charlie couldn't stop himself from flinching away—even though he knew it was Josh. "Shhh, it's okay, Charlie, I'm here. No one is going to hurt you now. I'm so fucking sorry I wasn't here." Josh managed to get Charlie sat up and banded his arms around him, rocking him where they sat on the sofa.

He didn't know how long they sat there, but once Charlie stopped shaking, he was able to breathe easier and think. Pushing against Josh's chest, he sat up and tried to compose himself. He took a breath, stood and, realising his trousers were still undone, quickly fastened them before heading to the bathroom.

"Charlie?" Josh called.

Charlie shut the door after him, not replying. He couldn't at that moment. He needed to regroup for a minute before facing Josh again. He stared at his reflection in the mirror, eyes roaming all over his own face. He knew Jimmy hadn't got too far, but it was still far enough to scare Charlie.

He knew he couldn't stay in there all night, so splashed his face with cold water, dried off and opened the door. Josh was sitting exactly where he'd left him. Charlie looked at his face and saw hopelessness, fear and anger. "I'm okay. He didn't get as far as he'd hoped. That's something at least."

"Who?" The word burst from Josh's lips in an angry blast of air.

Charlie looked down at the floor. "Jimmy."

13

Josh

"That asshole!" Josh was more furious than he had ever been in his entire eighteen years. How dare Jimmy do this to Charlie. He tried to calm down when he saw Charlie flinch with his outburst. Another mark against Jimmy. Charlie never used to flinch from anything, especially Josh. He had a lot to answer for. "You have to call the police, Charlie."

Charlie shook his head. "There's no point, there's no evidence of anything. It's going to be his word against mine."

"What about me? I can tell them how I found you when I came in."

Charlie shook his head again. "You're family, J. You know they won't listen. I'm so annoyed with myself because I usually lock the front door after the last customer. I could have sworn I'd done it tonight, but Jimmy got in, so I couldn't have."

"Don't you even put the blame for this on you," Josh said angrily. "None of this is your fault. It's all on him. Every last bit of it. I don't want to hear you blaming yourself for any of this. Do you understand?"

He could see Charlie trying to listen. "I know I should not be blaming myself. But it's difficult when I could have prevented this."

"Could you?" Josh said this quietly, which made Charlie look at him and listen. "Could you have prevented this? Maybe this particular scenario could have been, but what if Jimmy caught you at a different time or different place? I don't want to scare you more, but you need to think about it." Josh walked over to him, stopping within arm's reach. "If he hadn't attempted this now, he may have tried some other time."

Charlie looked away. "He threatened there would be a next time," he said so quietly Josh had to strain to hear.

Josh closed his eyes, crossed his arms on his chest and squeezed tight to stop from exploding. He didn't want to worry Charlie more than he already had done. He felt Charlie's hand on his arm and opened his eyes. Looking straight at Charlie, he said, "It's not your fault."

Josh saw the moment Charlie broke. He just moved his arms in time to catch him before he fell to the floor. Wrapping his arms around him, Josh took them to the floor carefully, keeping Charlie in the frame of his legs and rocking him. Josh didn't know how much more they could take. It was one thing after another at the moment.

A long while after Charlie had calmed, Josh moved, trying to encourage him to get up. "We need to get home." Josh cupped Charlie's cheek, seeing a vacant look in his eyes. That worried Josh.

Charlie pushed away from him slowly and rose. Without talking, they grabbed Charlie's coat and phone, then walked back towards the bar. As they passed by the back door, Charlie shuddered and walked quicker. Josh didn't have to wonder why. At the front door, Josh took the keys from Charlie and locked up under his direction. Turning, he handed the keys back to Charlie and wrapped his arm around his shoulder. They walked the short distance to Josh's car. There was no way he would let Charlie drive in this condition.

The drive home was quiet. The entry to home even quieter. Charlie walked straight up the stairs and into his room, shutting the door behind him without even a goodnight. Josh blew out a breath. He couldn't imagine what Charlie was going through, but he wished he could help him. *Tomorrow*, he thought. *I'll help him tomorrow.*

• • • ● ● • ● ● • • •

The next morning, having slept very little the previous night, Josh walked into the kitchen, saying good morning to his mum.

"Is Charlie up yet?" he asked as he got out some bread for toast.

"Didn't he tell you? He's gone out for the day." Mum smiled. "I told him it was about time he took some of the holiday time he was owed. Apparently, it was a short notice thing. He only decided this morning." His mum looked at Josh happily, not noticing the tension in his jaw.

Josh couldn't believe Charlie had up and left; it wasn't something Charlie would normally do. As Josh thought more though, he realised it would probably be for the best, and it would give Josh time to speak with Jimmy.

Trying for casual, he asked, "Oh, where has he gone? Somewhere nice I hope."

"Birmingham. You know how much he likes that aquarium. It will be nice for him to have some time to himself." His mum looked at him. "I know things are up in the air between you two, but I think it would be a good time for you both to think things through." She held up her hand to stop Josh from interrupting. "I know you know how you feel, Josh. But this will give you some time alone when you are not distracted by seeing him."

Josh thought about it. He nodded his head. He did agree with it in principle, but he was going to make sure he spoke to Charlie as much as he would allow. He didn't want to lose him because of Jimmy.

"Okay, I will," he promised.

After eating his breakfast, he went to his room to grab his phone and immediately messaged Charlie.

JOSH: *Hey, CB. Are you okay? I missed you this morning. x*

He wasn't expecting a reply any time soon. Knowing Charlie, he would wait to reply until he arrived where he was going. Josh pocketed his phone and got his things ready for college. Maybe he could get some information from people there.

Stalking his way through the streets, he arrived at college in record time. Ducking into the coffee shop, he ordered a coffee to go. As he waited, he saw Kent and Carla in the back corner. When he'd got his drink, he went over to speak with them.

"Hey, guys. How are you doing?" Josh stood by the table not wanting to interrupt for too long.

Carla looked at Josh, then down at the table, and Kent looked at him, eyebrows raised. "Hey, Josh. We're good thanks."

"I wanted to ask you something really quick. Have you seen anything of Jimmy lately?" Josh heard more noise coming behind him, the shop must have had an influx of customers. He looked over his shoulder and saw, yes, the shop did have more customers, but most of them were looking his way. Well, they were until he looked at them, then their eyes skipped away from him. He frowned and looked back at Kent, waiting for his answer.

"Look, man, I don't know what's going on, but it seems like you've had your head in your ass this past day." Kent picked up his phone and began tapping away at it. "I have a feeling you have not seen the photos that are going around." He pressed his phone a couple more times before handing it over to Josh.

Josh took it slowly, not sure if he wanted to see what was on it. Glancing down, his heart sank. There were four pictures altogether. The first showed Josh and Charlie outside the school entrance, locked in a kiss from the other day. The second photo was from a distance but was definitely him and Charlie sat in Charlie's window, arms around each other from when they'd found out Charlie was adopted. The third showed the walking side by side, outside the bar, with Josh's arm around Charlie's shoulder and him kissing his forehead from last night. But the one that got him so blindingly angry was the picture of Charlie, splayed out of the sofa in the bar with his trousers around his knees, ass and legs on display. Stamped across it were the words 'Jimmy's bitch'.

"Where the fuck are these from?" Josh demanded with barely restrained control. "Who put them out there?"

Kent looked him in the eye. "I don't know where it started from, but several people received emails this morning with the photos attached, and then it spread from there. You know what social media is like, Josh. You need to be careful."

Josh leaned down close to Kent, his voice deadly quiet. "You listen to me good, Kent. Two of those photos had completely innocent reasons and have been completely taken out of context. The third, I will not explain to anyone as of yet. As for 'Jimmy's bitch'," Josh said making air quotes with his fingers, "that was taken when Jimmy tried to rape Charlie last night. And he would've done had I not walked in to take Charlie home. Now you make damn sure, you get all the facts before saying anything like that to me again." Josh got really close. "Do you understand me?"

Kent didn't back off but searched Josh's face for a minute, before nodding. "Sorry, Josh. It came as a shock, and I jumped to conclusions."

"You're damn right, you did." Josh shook his head. "Can you send me those pictures, including where you got it from? I may need it as evidence."

"Where's Charlie? This is going to destroy him." Kent focused on sending the images through.

"He's gone away for the day, which now couldn't have worked out better." Josh took out his phone at the notification sound and saw Kent's message. "Got them, thanks. There are some things you don't know, Kent, and I'm going to ask a favour. I've known you for a long while, and I'm hoping I can count on you to back me up. I know you'd be doing this on faith alone, but I will explain everything as soon as I can. I need to sort some things out first. Can you do that?"

Kent didn't answer straight away, but Carla piped up, "Definitely." Josh looked at her in surprise. "I'm going to believe what you're saying is true because I've known you for years, and I've never known you to lie to us. We will need an explanation soon, but for now, let us know if we can help."

Josh smiled at her, gratefully. "Thanks, Carla. That means a lot. At the moment, the only thing I need is to know where Jimmy is." Then he had a thought. "Son of a bitch!" He grabbed his head with his hands.

"What's the matter?" Kent asked.

"Aiden," Josh said as if it explained everything, which it did to him, just not to Kent and Carla. "Aiden has been blackmailing me to keep our relationship going or he was going to release one of the photos. That's why you saw us that day in the café. I was there under duress, trying to protect Charlie from any repercussions of the photo. I should have remembered straight away he'd threatened to leak them."

"Well, I've not seen him so far today."

"He's probably hiding out. I'm gonna kick his ass when I see him." Josh became aware of the noise behind him again. "My day is turning to shit. This is going to be a nightmare."

Kent and Carla rose to stand with him. "We'll come with you. They'll tear you to pieces if you're alone."

"No, don't worry about it. I don't want any of this rubbing off on you two. If it's okay, I'll message you if I need anything? Or you message me if you hear any more? I doubt anything will get sent to me."

"Are you sure, man?"

"Yeah, don't worry. I'll be fine. See you later." Josh turned and walked to the door, the crowd shrinking away from him as he strode passed them. This is going to be one long-ass day. He sighed. He threw his coffee cup in the bin as it had gone cold during the conversation with Kent.

Josh couldn't believe Aiden had the balls to leak those photos. He was a little concerned about the two pictures from last night. He assumed those had been taken by Jimmy, which means Aiden and Jimmy were working together if all the photos had been leaked at the same time.

He grabbed his phone and dialled Charlie's number. It rang for a long few seconds before he picked up.

"Hi." Charlie's voice was quiet.

"Hi. Are you okay?" Josh asked. It was the main question he needed an answer to right now.

"Yeah, I'm okay. Sorry, I left without saying anything."

"No worries, I understand why you did. Something else has happened though, and I wasn't sure if you'd found out or not. Some pictures have been released." Josh waited to see what Charlie would say.

"What pictures?" Charlie sounded confused.

"Pictures of you and me...and another one." Josh didn't want to bring that specific picture up but knew it would be better to warn Charlie rather than wait until he saw it.

"Wait, what? Who got pictures of us? And how?" Charlie's voice was rising in panic.

"Charlie, calm down. Let me explain what I know." Josh took a deep breath. "There are four pictures being sent on social media and emails. Three of them are of you and me. Outside the college, through your bedroom window after we'd found out about the adoption and the third outside the bar last night. All of them together—out of context—paint a decidedly unfortunate story."

"Jesus Christ. Who the hell did that?"

"I have a feeling it was Aiden and Jimmy."

They were both silent for the moment, lost in thought, before Charlie spoke again. "I should have made the connection before." Charlie's voice got louder as he explained about seeing Jimmy and Aiden together near the cinema, then Jimmy being outside of it when they came out, and finally, Jimmy's parting words last night. "Jimmy mentioned something about Aiden being patient enough to wait. I had no idea what he was talking about. Hang on a minute. Some of this is clicking now. Tom mentioned yesterday about a guy called Travis who keeps ringing asking to be taken on as the manager. Obviously, Tom kept telling him there wasn't a position available. Jimmy also mentioned last night he had an acquaintance who wanted his brother in the position. That means this Travis guy is probably Aiden's brother." Charlie blew out a breath. "Jimmy implied this was all happening because Aiden wants his brother to manage Crush. Oh, he also said Aiden was trying to keep someone close to him."

Josh's laugh was not humorous at all. "Yeah, that would be me."

"What?"

"Aiden has been blackmailing me to stay in a relationship with him. Something to do with me being the perfect face for him to have on his arm. He was the one who took the photo of us outside the college. When he came to me with the photo, I folded. I didn't want it to come back on you."

"Josh. You shouldn't have done that. We could have explained it away somehow. God, this is a mess. I'll head back now."

"No!" Josh stopped Charlie. "As much as I would love for you to come home, stay where you are. Give me some time to sort something out or find out more information or something. You may as well try and get some rest in while you're there. Ring Ginny, talk to her. Tell her everything. She'll understand." Josh hoped she would at least.

"Okay. Keep me in the loop though, alright. Don't do anything stupid."

"No guarantees there." Josh chuckled. "I'll speak to you later."

"Okay. Bye—wait! You said four photos. What was the other one of?" Josh closed his eyes against the pain he knew he was about to inflict on Charlie. Subconsciously he had hoped Charlie would forget about the fourth one, but Josh knew he needed to be prepared.

"It's...not good, Charlie."

"Tell me."

"I'm sorry. It's a photo of you as I found you last night, with some demeaning words as well."

Josh heard a thump through the phone, and he started shouting for Charlie. "Charlie! Are you okay? Charlie! Charlie!" He heard more noise then Charlie's voice came back.

"I have to go. I'll call you later." Then the phone went dead.

Josh dialled Ginny's number.

"Hey, Josh."

"Hey, Ginny. I need your help. I need you to try and call Charlie. Talk to him, Gin. He has a hell of a lot of information to give you, and I need you to be strong for him and stand by him, regardless. I know I'm asking a lot of you because you'd be agreeing to do this without any information. But please, I beg you, stay with him through all of the crap which is coming our way."

Ginny was silent for a short time. "Okay. I'm taking a lot on blind faith, but neither of you has ever hurt me in the past. I will stand by him regardless of what he tells me. I promise. I need to talk to him anyway."

"Have you seen the photos which have come out?"

"No, nothing, why?" she said.

"They're bad, Gin. One in particular show more than Charlie would ever want anyone to see. That's what I told him. I wanted him to be prepared in case they came through to him. He went straight off the phone. Try and call him for me, check he's okay. I didn't mean to hurt him."

"I will. I'll call him now."

Josh blew out a breath in relief. At least Charlie would have someone to look after him and help him through the rollercoaster emotions. "Thanks. I'll speak to you soon."

He hung up the phone, realising he had a small audience. "What?" he shouted at them and stalked towards his first class of the day. Entering the classroom, all conversations stopped. The tutor approached him and quietly asked for a word. They stepped outside.

"Mr Reynolds would like to speak with you in the office please, Josh. He asked me to tell you to head straight over there." His tutor looked sympathetic and patted his shoulder as he walked back into the class. Josh stood there for a moment, then turned and headed towards the office. No point guessing what this was about.

14

Charlie

Charlie sat in the window seat of the aquarium cafe cradling a cup of hot tea. He stared out the window, mind going in circles around everything that was going on. He couldn't seem to figure out what to do. After Josh's phone call, Charlie had managed to find his way to the café and requested tea. The waitress had tried to talk to him, but he wasn't able to get his thoughts together enough for conversation, so she had left him to it.

He couldn't get over the fact there was a photo out there of him nearly naked. It was bad enough remembering he'd heard a click and not knowing what it was, but now knowing it must have been Jimmy's camera? That was much worse, naturally. It would have never even crossed his mind Jimmy would have done something like that.

He'd been over that night again and again in his head, trying to remember everything that happened. He didn't want to, but he knew there was something they were missing. He couldn't figure out why Jimmy was helping Aiden. It couldn't be because he wanted to sleep with Charlie. That seemed too simple.

Charlie shook his head, his thoughts returning to that photo. He hadn't seen it yet, but he could imagine what it looked like.

Imagine what *he* looked like. And to also remember Josh had seen him like it—it was so humiliating.

He heard his phone ring and looked to see it was Ginny. He blew out a breath.

Charlie stayed quiet for a moment before answering. "Hey, Gin," he waited until she replied, then said quietly, "I have a lot to tell you."

"I know, Charlie Bear. Take your time."

Charlie hugged himself tight. "Thank you." He wiped at his eyes. He looked up startled as a cup was put in front of him. The waitress had placed a mug of hot chocolate in front of him.

"You looked like you needed something to cheer you up. On the house." She smiled and walked away. Charlie stared after her, then at the creamy hot chocolate, squirty cream, chocolate flakes and marshmallows. His favourite.

"Charlie?" Ginny's voice roused him.

"Sorry. I'm okay. The waitress brought me a hot chocolate to keep me company." Cradling the warm mug, he tried to decide where to start. "Remember we had the conversation about Mum and Dad being separated and not telling us?" He waited for her agreement. "Well, they had another secret they told us yesterday. I'm adopted." He used a spoon to scoop some cream off the top of his hot chocolate, allowing the news to sink in.

"What?" Ginny shouted through the phone. "What the hell?"

"Yeah. Mum told us she was informed she couldn't conceive, so went through the adoption process. Two months after they had adopted me, they found out she was pregnant with Josh." Charlie took a sip, then placed the mug on the table. "I don't really know how to talk about this so I'm going to blurt it out. I've done some things with Josh." Charlie blushed, even though she couldn't see him and, before he lost the nerve, quickly added, "Sexual things."

Ginny was silent for a moment. "I don't quite know what to say," she said quietly.

Charlie cleared his throat. "I'd been having these thoughts about him for a while but had been telling myself to ignore them. I would never have acted on them."

"So, you did once you found out about the adoption? Wait, no that was only yesterday…" Ginny stopped herself.

"No, the night of the date with Jimmy. Josh blames himself for it, but it wasn't his fault. Not just his fault anyway. We got talking about how I still hadn't been kissed, and he was comforting me. I went to pull away as I felt I was getting too close. Physically and emotionally. He held me tight and then asked if he could kiss me." Charlie wiped at the tears running down his face. He continued in a whisper, "I knew it was wrong, we both did. But I so wanted it, so I said yes." He cupped a hand over his mouth, stifling his sob.

"Shh, it's okay, it's okay. God, I wish I was there with you. I'm not saying I understand this, but I'm here, and I'm not going anywhere." Charlie cried harder at that. He grabbed some napkins from the dispenser on the table.

After a short time, Charlie was able to compose himself enough to continue. "We went further than kissing but not sex. Josh pulled himself apart afterwards, taking all the blame, but I couldn't let him. There were two of us there. The next time it happened when I was getting ready for work one night, Josh came in without knocking—as we always had I might add—and I was only half-dressed. He was so giving, so careful with me."

"You slept together?" Ginny asked.

"No, no. We haven't slept together at all. He gave me a blowjob." Charlie looked around, keeping his voice quiet, then looked down at his hands, embarrassed. "The night we found out about Mum and Dad's separation, Josh was broken. You know what I said he was like the day after? Well, this was just as bad. He was so angry. We slept in his bed, just sleeping, until the morning when…never mind. After Josh called me away from shopping with you, he kissed me outside college. It was only a small kiss, but it shouldn't have happened in public. That's what one of the photos was of. Aiden had seen us and taken a photo, then used it as blackmail material to make Josh stay in a relationship with him."

Charlie reached forward for his mug and took a sip. "After his breakdown, Josh came to work with me, so he didn't have to stay at home. He got drunk. I let him sleep on the sofa in the office while I finished my shift. When everyone had gone and I'd cleaned up, I went back to check on him. He was fast asleep but said my name." Charlie shook his head again. "I shouldn't have...but I couldn't resist." Charlie blew out another breath. Ginny didn't say anything, probably wanting him to get it all out before she freaked out.

"Another of the photos was taken of Josh comforting me in my bedroom window after being told about the adoption. It was taken completely out of context, but it's damning enough with the other one. Then, last night, Jimmy happened." Charlie stiffened up, not wanting to go through this out loud but knowing he had to. "After everyone had left the bar, I began to clean knowing I had to wait for Josh to meet me there before leaving. I did what Tom asked and made sure I wouldn't go home alone. I thought I'd locked the front door, but Jimmy appeared."

Charlie began to rub his hands together when they started shaking. He took some deep breaths, trying to stem the flow of tears again. "He told me about Aiden's plan to get his brother to take over managing Crush, then said...he'd come to collect." Charlie was panting now. "He grabbed me and managed to get me in the back office. Throwing me on to the sofa on my stomach and pulling my trousers down—" Charlie broke off as he could hardly breathe. Saying it out loud was different to replaying it in his head. In his head, he could separate himself. Out loud he knew it had been done to him and it took a bigger toll.

"Shit, Charlie. Did he rape you?" Ginny's voice was strained as if holding back tears as well.

Charlie tried to calm his breathing so he could finish the story. "Josh arrived before he could do anything more than expose me. I hadn't realised at the time, but Jimmy managed to take a photo of me in that compromising position. That is another of the photos. It's the one Josh didn't want to tell me about. The one that made me—"

"—break," Ginny finished. Charlie nodded, even though she couldn't see him.

"After Josh found me, he looked after me and took me home. The final photo was taken out of context again because it was Josh with his arm around my shoulders after the attack." Charlie blew out a big breath. "That's you up to date, I think." Charlie tried for a chuckle, but it fell a little flat.

"Jesus, Charlie. You've been through hell." She blew out a breath. "I wish you'd have come to me. I don't claim to understand your relationship with Josh, but I'm still your friend."

"I know you are. I'm so confused about everything and it seemed like everything was piling up and piling up, and I just...couldn't. But being my friend is why I rang you this morning about coming here. I needed to get away. Although I thought it was a lot before I found out about the photos. That's added even more pressure now."

"Do you want to look at the photos?" she asked, carefully.

Charlie shook his head. "Not at the moment. Maybe eventually, when I can't get away from them. But not now."

"Fair enough."

Charlie felt much lighter now he'd spoken to Ginny. He'd not worked through anything as yet but maybe the quote about sharing is halving may have juice to it.

The waitress returned, sympathy showing in her eyes. "Sorry to interrupt. Would you like some lunch?" It was early, but it gave him something to distract himself with.

"Could I have some soup and bread please?" he asked, his voice hoarse.

"Of course. I'll bring it out shortly."

It was so peaceful here. Charlie was sure Ginny had lots to think about, so he kept quiet for a short time.

"Do you love him?" Ginny asked suddenly.

Charlie startled at the question. Did he? Was he was attracted to the fact Josh was unattainable? Did he want a relationship with him? Could he have a relationship with him? There were so many questions which didn't have answers to them. But that one did, and Ginny seemed to realise it. "Yes." Such a simple response, but it would make a huge difference in their lives. "I don't know if I can deal with the stigma it would generate. I bet there is enough of it now towards Josh, but even if the adoption came out and Josh wanted a relationship, there would always those people who'd remind others of us being brothers. I don't know if I can do it."

Charlie looked down at his hands, ashamed. He wasn't strong like Josh was. He would prefer to hide away from confrontations and gossip, whereas Josh would let it go or put in his two cents.

"I'm jumping the gun anyway. Josh hasn't even mentioned anything about feelings or the future. Last time I saw him, after the attack, I pushed him away and didn't speak to him until that phone call earlier."

"That can be a topic for discussion another day. The first thing you need to decide is if you're going to press charges on Jimmy. You have evidence it happened." When Charlie voiced his confusion, she added, "The photo. It shows you both were there. The only difficulty is proving it wasn't consensual."

"I can't press charges, Gin. The police will have to see the other photos as well. There will be too much to try and explain away. I don't want to put us all through it unless I have to."

"Okay, well let's table it for now then. Second thing, we need to find out who sent those photos and get them taken down."

"As much as I would love that, I don't think there is any point to it. They will be everywhere by now. I don't know if taking the first ones down will remove the rest." Charlie sighed and scratched his head. There didn't seem to be any solutions to the problems he had.

"Thirdly, we need to find out what we can about Aiden's brother from Tom. He mentioned to me he'd been receiving phone calls from this Travis guy. I'll give him a call and find out what else he knows about him." She paused. "Am I able to tell him some things?"

Charlie took a breath and let it go slowly. Eventually, everyone was going to find out anyway, and he supposed it would be better if Tom knew first. "Tell him everything. I hope he's as open-minded as you have been." He continued, "Thank you, Ginny, from the bottom of my heart. Thank you."

She told him to shut up, making him laugh, and went off to call Tom.

He hated there was a chance he could lose his job, but he held out hope Ginny could reason with Tom if it happened. He also hoped this would all go away.

15

Josh

Josh stood outside the office after having spoken with the Head. Mr Reynolds had informed him he'd been made aware of the photos circulating and was disgusted by the people who had done it. He said it would be looked into but had requested Josh take a leave of absence for a short time while the investigation took place.

Josh hadn't wanted to, but Mr Reynolds insisted. He hadn't wanted to argue too much because Mr Reynolds had never actually said anything else about the photos. He hadn't wanted or needed, to know whether they were true or not, and he certainly hadn't made any derogatory comments. Which, of course, as Head, he shouldn't make, but that doesn't mean the words don't get said.

He was surprised by the support he seemed to be getting from him, but it still didn't change the fact Josh didn't want to stop coming to college. He thought it seemed like he was in the wrong and hiding out, when in fact he was happy in a way.

And he felt awful because he felt happy. It meant his relationship with Charlie was free from being hidden. He could talk about it and not have to worry about saying something wrong. Yes, people were going to be weird about it, but he didn't care. One downside to this was the picture of Charlie. That had made Josh so angry, he had very nearly exploded with rage, but he couldn't find one of the two people who deserved it. They were in hiding, he bet. And they better bloody hide because if he found them, they were in deep shit.

Josh started walking home, then decided to do a detour to Crush. If he wasn't at college, maybe he could get some extra work experience at the bar if Tom let him. It would certainly help Josh out, but it may help Tom out, too, as he would be one bartender short with Charlie being away.

It took him about half an hour to walk to the bar. He found it closed as it was early morning, but he remembered Charlie saying Tom usually worked on paperwork during the closed hours, so he might still be there.

Josh knocked on the door, waiting if a little impatiently. He knocked again louder when there was no answer. After a few minutes, he decided to go to the back door and see if he had any luck there. Tom might not even be there. Walking down the alley, he stopped at the door and knocked loudly, the noise echoing in the small area.

He heard muffled noises coming from inside, then Tom opened the door looking annoyed until he saw who it was. He stared at him for a moment, mobile held to his ear, then opened the door wider for Josh to enter.

"I know what you're saying. It's a lot to take in." Tom paused his side of the conversation. "Yeah, I do know him. He wouldn't go into this lightly. Okay, well Josh has turned up, so I'll speak with him and call you back later, okay?" He paused again. "Bye."

Tom blew out a breath and hung up the phone. He looked down at it for a short time, before blowing out a breath and looking at Josh. "You've got yourselves into a right jam, haven't you?" He shook his head. "Follow me. I think I'm going to need alcohol for this conversation." Tom headed towards the bar, Josh following obediently.

Josh had a feeling he knew who had been on the phone and what had been discussed. He hoped this was going to go the way he expected it to. Tom didn't seem like someone who would disown him because he didn't follow true to form, but it was also a lot to ask of him.

Tom grabbed the bottle of whiskey and two glasses, placing them on the bar before pouring a small bit in each. Sliding one glass to Josh, he took his own and swallowed it in one go. Wincing, Josh followed suit, coughing as it burned his throat. He'd never had whiskey before and wasn't sure he would again.

Tom laughed and took the glass from Josh, grabbing him a beer instead.

"Thanks." Josh sat on the opposite side of the bar, watching Tom as he poured himself another whiskey. "You got your head around it yet?" Josh asked.

Tom looked at him, shaking his head. "A lot to take in. Give me a few minutes to process, while we talk about why you came."

Josh glanced at him for a minute, then nodded. "I was coming to ask whether I could get some work experience here for a while. With everything that's happened, the Head has told me to take a leave of absence while the photos are investigated. I thought I would take the time to help you out as well as myself. I understand if you don't want me to though." Josh refused to look away.

Tom looked at him, the silence tense, then nodded his head. "Sounds like a plan. Do you want to come in tonight? I can get Analise or Rob to show you some bits."

Josh smiled. "Great, thanks." He paused. "You have any questions?"

Tom laughed out loud. "Fuck loads! But I need to keep reminding myself you're not related by blood." He sighed loudly. "I'm going to be honest with you. It's taking a lot to get rid of my initial disgust. I keep reminding myself I know you both really well, and

I have to separate you in my head; otherwise, I can't cope with it. I won't ever get in your face or in your way or anything like that. But it's difficult. You understand?"

Josh nodded. "Yeah, more than you realise."

• • • • • • • • • • •

Josh walked the long route home, making a call to Charlie as he walked.

"Hey, you. You doing okay?"

"Yeah, not too bad. I told Ginny everything. Absolutely everything. And she's still here for us, so I guess that means we have some support." Charlie sighed.

"I've just left Tom. We have his support, too, although it's taking him some time to digest it all, understandably." Josh thought Tom would come around eventually, it would just take some time.

"Yeah. Why did you go to Crush in the first place?" Charlie asked.

Josh told him about the visit to the Head of the college and about going to Tom to ask if he could do the work experience with him.

"That's a brilliant idea! Analise, Rob and I will have you trained in no time." Charlie laughed.

They were both silent for a while, lots of things being said without words. Then Charlie broke it. "Have you seen or heard anything from Aiden or Jimmy?"

"No, neither were showing their faces anywhere I saw today, and the few people I asked, either didn't know or didn't tell me. I'm heading home now. I'm going to speak to Dad to see if he can give me any advice. I know it's not ideal, but they were really supportive when they both found out if you think about it."

"Do you have to tell them about last night?" he asked so quietly, Josh almost didn't catch it.

"I think I need to, but what I will do is explain the other photos first, and then I will only tell him if I absolutely have to. I'm sorry Charlie, I know you wouldn't want them to know, but I really think I have to tell them." Josh's heart broke because he knew how torn up Charlie was about people knowing what happened to him. He wasn't sure whether Charlie would need some psychological help once this was all over or whether he would be fine without it. Well, he had Josh for support. And Ginny and Tom. And their parents. He hoped it would be enough.

Josh heard a sniffle on the other end of the line. "I know. I wish they didn't have to know."

"Me, too, Charlie. Me, too." Josh's eyes were wet and his voice thick with tears. "I miss you, pipsqueak." Josh smiled, remembering the messages from what seemed like ages ago.

Charlie laughed as much as he could. "I miss you, buttbrain."

Josh saw his house come into view and told Charlie he was almost there.

"Okay, I'll speak to you later." They hung up.

Josh entered the house, calling for Mum and Dad, but no one answered. He went through the rooms, stalling in the kitchen when he saw a note on the fridge saying,

At the Bennetts' house, we'll be back for dinner, love M & D x

Josh trudged upstairs to his room. The conversation would have to wait until later. Maybe he could get some painting done while it was quiet. He rummaged around in his cupboard to find his supplies and took them into the conservatory to work. It had better natural light there making it easier to see the different shades of colour.

He placed the first canvas on his easel and began mixing some colours. He didn't have any idea of what was going to come of it, but he would just paint and see what the result was. He did this sometimes, firstly, because it helped him to relax and think, and secondly, because the result was usually pretty good when he didn't agonise so much over it.

• • • ● ●•● ● • • •

Josh answered his phone, distractedly. "Hello?"

"Hey, J. I've got a bit of a problem."

"What's the matter?"

"My car won't start. I asked someone to help me jump it but it's completely dead. I've called the breakdown, but because it's getting late, they don't think the garage will be able to look at it tonight." Charlie sounded miserable.

"Shit. Okay, do you want me to come down for you?" Josh asked.

"No, don't worry. I don't want to leave my car here, then have to come back for it. I'm going to get a hotel room for the night and see what the garage says when it gets dropped off there tonight." Charlie blew out a breath. "I'm going to call Mum after this and let them know I won't be home for dinner."

Josh told Charlie their parents were out until later. "I'll let them know when they get back, don't worry."

"That was fast. The breakdown guy is here. I'll call you back when I get to the hotel, I'll hopefully know more about timings then."

"Okay, Charlie, speak to you later."

"Bye."

Josh put his phone down after disconnecting. His eyes took in the painting he had made. It was coming together nicely. There were lots of dark blues, blacks and streaks of dark green. It reminded him of Charlie, he realised. Those were the colours Charlie liked to wear, so it made sense that they were reminiscent of him.

He picked up his paintbrush and started again, thinking about the phone call and hoping Charlie was alright. Soon, he got lost in the motions.

"Josh! We're home!" his mum shouted. Josh blinked his eyes, tuning in to what was being said. "Is Charlie home yet?"

He put down his brush and walked into the kitchen. "No, he rang..." Josh looked at the clock, seeing another hour had passed, "...an hour ago and said he'd had car trouble. The breakdown had just arrived so I'm waiting for a call back. He said he was going to stay at a hotel tonight."

"Why? Can the garage not fix it?" his dad asked.

"He doesn't know, but he thinks it will be too late now for them to do anything. He'll call back later with more information." Josh went to the sink to wash his hands but, realising he had paint everywhere, decided to head for a shower instead. "I'm going to go for a shower before dinner if that's okay? I didn't realise how messy I'd gotten."

Mum laughed. "That's fine. I'll call you when dinner's ready."

Josh ran up the stairs to his bedroom. As he stripped off, his phone rang again. Charlie. "Hey, how's it going?"

"Okay. The garage said they wouldn't have time to fit it in tonight, so I'm at a hotel now." Charlie sounded tired, but Josh knew how to make him feel better.

"Are you in your room?" Josh asked, still in his jeans.

"Yes, why?" Charlie asked.

"I'm in my room." He got comfy on his bed, arm behind his head, uncaring of getting paint everywhere. "I'm going to help you relax a little."

"What do you want to do?" Charlie was sounding more confused by the minute. Josh was going to shock him.

"I want to have phone sex." Josh was so matter of fact, but Charlie's response made him laugh out loud.

"WHAT! No way! We can't do that! No way, J, not happening." Charlie was adamant, but Josh was determined he would do this for Charlie. He needed to let off some steam and relax a little before everything else came tumbling back into his brain. It might not be the best thing to do in the circumstances, especially as Charlie had left to get some space, but Josh believed he needed it. They both did.

"Yes, way. Lock the door and take your clothes off." Josh chuckled at the way Charlie sputtered his refusal. "Now Charlie!" Josh's voice got firm.

He heard Charlie's intake of breath and the shaking quality of his exhale, then he heard some noise on the other end before a distinct click of a door locking.

"I don't know if I can." Charlie seemed so beaten down at that point Josh nearly reconsidered.

"You can. You need to relax. I'm not going to hurt you or make you do something you don't want to do. I promise. I want to make you feel good." Josh was careful with his words. He didn't want to push too much and make Charlie baulk completely. There was silence on the line, so Josh waited for Charlie to make a decision.

"Wait a moment." Josh heard the bump of the phone being put down. After a minute or two, he heard it be picked up again. "I'm ready," Charlie whispered.

Josh closed his eyes and smiled. "Okay, there are always some complimentary items somewhere. Try the bathroom and see if they have some lotion amongst the little bottles." He heard noises on the other side.

"I've got some."

"Perfect. Take it to the bed with you and lie down. Close your eyes and listen to my voice, picture me there with you. You're lying on your back, and I'm laying right next to you on my side, head resting on my hand as my other rests on your chest. Put your hand there, Charlie. Feel how smooth your skin is. It's like silk. I'm moving my hand in small circles closer to your nipples. I smooth a finger around your nipple not quite touching it."

Josh heard Charlie's small gasp. "That's it. Now I'm moving it over the top gently, not pressing but making it bead. Flick your nail over it, Charlie, feel how hard it is and then soothe it with your finger." Charlie gasped again. "Move over to the other nipple now and do the same. Both are hard points now and need my mouth, but your hands will have to do. Lick your fingertip and wet your nub." Josh was so hard, he didn't know if he had the patience to take this very far. But he would try, for Charlie.

"Mmmm, oh!" Charlie made a surprised noise.

"Are you moving your wet finger over your nipple, Charlie?" he asked.

"Ye-yeah! It feels so good, Josh."

"I can make you feel better. Put the phone on speaker and rest it next to your head on the pillow." Josh heard a muffle, then silence until he heard Charlie's breathing again.

"Okay."

"Right, keep one hand playing with your nipple and move the other hand slowly down your stomach. Small circles again, feel the softness of your skin. I love how you feel under my fingers and my mouth. Nothing tastes better." Josh undid his jeans and pushed them and his underwear under his cock. Sighing at the freedom, he wrapped his hand around his cock, giving it a slow stroke. He stopped immediately—he was already so close. "Slide your hand to your hip and then over to the other side, slowly."

"Ah! Josh, it's too much." Charlie sounded completely lost to the sensations.

"You're okay, Charlie. Move to your other nipple now, make sure you swap. Stroke your hand to your balls. Cup them and roll them in your hand." Josh moved his hand to his balls, doing exactly what he'd told Charlie to do. "Spread your legs for me,

Charlie. Now, reach your finger behind them and use your nail to graze over your taint."

"Oh, shit! Josh! I'm so hard. I want...oh...please, Josh!" Charlie sounded like he couldn't take much more, and Josh had to remind himself he wasn't as experienced as Josh was.

"Charlie, put your hand on the base of your cock. Squeeze it a little to take the edge off." Josh did the same, he felt like a newbie all over again. It was all to do with Charlie though. Everything seemed brand new with him.

"Oh, fuck, fuck! My nipples are aching!"

"Good. Get some of the lotion on your hand." He heard Charlie fumbling around. "Now stroke your hand up and down your cock. You want to be able to move easily."

He heard Charlie cry out, "Oh fuck! Josh! Oh god!"

Josh took hold of his cock again. "Can you feel my hands on your cock, Charlie? I'm holding it tight and pumping my hand. As I get to your tip, I'm rubbing under the tip of your cock, twisting my hand around as I bring it to the base again. I'm holding firmer now as I move my hand up, swiping my palm across the head."

"Josh! It feels so good!" Josh could hear Charlie panting.

"My mouth is on your nipples, getting them wet and hard, flicking the nub with my tongue. Your cock is so hard, Charlie." Josh was gasping now, finding it harder and harder to talk. "God! Move your hand up and down, twist gently as you reach under the edge of your tip, rub the underside and cup the tip then back down. Keep going, Charlie."

"Fuck, Josh, I'm not gonna last. Let me come! Please, Josh! Ah!"

"Fuck, Charlie, you are so hot. I want to watch you come all over your stomach. Move your hand faster now. Use your fingertips to massage the underside, up and down, quickly in short motions. Shift your other hand to cup your balls and graze behind them. Fuck! Come, Charlie, come!" Josh whisper-shouted the final command before his orgasm began to spill out of him.

"Josh!" He distantly heard Charlie panting his way through his own orgasm before coming back to the present. He'd not come that hard, ever. He blew out a breath, trying to get back to a normal rhythm. God, he was spent. That was so hot. He told Charlie as much.

Charlie didn't reply, to begin with. Then he chuckled, "Yeah, very hot." He paused. "Uh, and very messy."

Josh laughed. He looked down at himself and agreed. "But so worth it."

"Shit, Josh. I wasn't expecting that when I rang." Charlie sighed, seemingly content for the moment.

"Yeah, well. Why not when we have the time?" Josh laughed again. "How are you feeling?"

"Tired, but relaxed." Charlie snorted. "You certainly deliver what you say!"

"Yes, I do, Charlie. Yes, I do."

They talked for a few more minutes before Charlie complained of the cold stickiness on his stomach. They rang off hesitantly, Josh wanting to say something more than goodbye but not wanting to push Charlie too hard.

"Bye, Charlie Bear," Josh says, purposefully using Ginny's nickname and earning a chuckle from Charlie.

"Bye, J."

16

Josh

"I bet you feel better after that shower. How was college?" Josh came through to the kitchen and kissed his mum on the cheek, then went to sit at the table.

Josh sighed. "Not brilliant, Mum. Can I sit down and talk to you and Dad for a minute?"

His mum looked at him in concern. "Of course. John! Can you come in here please?" she called to his dad and sat down next to Josh. His dad came in and sat opposite him.

"What's up, son?" he asked.

"Well, there's a couple of things really. Firstly, and you're not going to be happy about this, but you also need to know, there have been some photos leaked online of Charlie and me. Two of them were completely innocent and taken out of context, the other was a kiss." Josh looked down at his hands. He couldn't bear to see whatever emotion was on their faces. "Because of this, Mr Reynolds has asked me to take a leave of absence from college until the investigation has finished." He scratched his nose, a nervous gesture.

"Is that why Charlie has gone?" his mum asked quietly.

"No, no. He went away before they came out. Charlie needs to get his head on straight, that's why he went."

"You said there were a couple of things?" his dad prompted.

"Yeah, I've asked Tom if I can work at the bar to get experience while I'm not at college. Hope that's okay?" Josh did look up then.

Mum patted his hand, distractedly. "Of course, sweetheart, that's fine."

"Also, there are two other people who know the full story about me and Charlie. Ginny and Tom. I told Charlie to tell Ginny so he'd have someone to talk to. And Ginny and Tom are together; therefore, Charlie told her to tell him so she didn't have to keep secrets from him. In hindsight, it makes my life at the bar a little easier too."

"Does the college have any ideas where the photos came from?" his dad asked a question Josh would have to be very careful answering if he didn't want to give too much away.

"Not at the moment, no. I have an idea and I've been trying to speak to the peop-person, but I've not seen them today." Josh fiddled with the sleeve of his jumper but stopped when he realised what he was doing.

"That's not everything is it?" His mother was far too observant.

"No," he said slowly, "but the rest is small compared to what I've said and nothing I can't handle." He winced at the lie he'd told his parents.

If his mother caught his wince, she didn't acknowledge it. "We trust you. You know where we are if you need us," she said. "What do you need from us now?"

"To be honest, I needed a sounding board. I can't figure out what to do about it, or if to do anything." That wasn't quite true, but he wanted to know what their thoughts were.

His dad sat back in his chair, stroking his chin as he thought. "I would leave everything to the college for the moment. Go to work at the bar, stay away from college and see what happens." He paused. "You could always have a word with that lawyer Charlie always mentions? Is it John-something?"

"Yeah. I'd forgotten. He goes to the bar quite a lot, so I might see him there. I'm heading to the bar after dinner." Yes, he would definitely ask him for advice if he saw him.

* * * * * * * * * *

Josh walked into the bar just before seven as he'd agreed with Tom earlier. He wouldn't be working until close, but he'd do a good four or five hours. He was ready for it, even a little excited. He understood why Charlie enjoyed it so much, especially seeing and hearing the atmosphere. It wasn't so ear-splitting you couldn't hear yourself think but noisy enough you had to talk louder than usual. He was beginning to love it.

"Hey, Josh!" Analise waved over the bar at him and smiled. "I hear you've come to join the team."

"Yep, no getting rid of me now!" He laughed.

"Yeah, we'll see about that. Hey Rob! Come here." Analise motioned the other bartender over. "This is Charlie's brother, Josh. He's come to get some hands-on training." Josh winced when he heard the word brother but kept his smile in place and reached out a hand to shake.

"Hey, Josh, nice to meet you." He took his hand back and walked back over to where he had been standing.

"Don't mind him. He's awesome but very focused on what he's doing. You'll be with me tonight. Come on around."

Josh walked behind the counter and put on an apron. For the next hour, he shadowed Analise, learning the ropes and trying to remember different drink concoctions. That part was not as easy. Luckily, they had a list which detailed every drink and what went into it, including amounts. He decided he would take that home one day and learn it all so he didn't have to keep referring to it.

He looked out across the bar, seeing everyone having fun and realising he wasn't feeling like he was missing out by being on the opposite side of the bar. He still felt involved, which he hadn't expected to. Out of the corner of his eye, he saw the door open and a few guys come in. He took a glance and saw Johnson. After he finished the drinks he was making, he asked Analise if he could have a few minutes to go speak to him.

"Sure, you've done well. Get your ass back in fifteen. It'll be time then for you to try solo for a few while I take a break." She smiled wickedly at him.

Josh laughed. "If you're sure I'm ready, I'll do my best. Thanks." He walked over to Johnson's group. "Hey, Johnson, have you got a minute?"

Johnson turned, smiling when he saw Josh, then his eyes narrowed when he saw Josh's face. "Of course." Josh walked towards the office in the back, knowing Tom wouldn't mind letting him use it for a short time.

After asking if he wanted a drink, Josh sat down next to Johnson and started detailing the problems. He had to fully disclose everything to him, but he knew Johnson would keep it confidential. After explaining about him and Charlie, all he got was an eyebrow raise, so he carried on explaining about the adoption, Jimmy's attempted rape, the photos, college trying to investigate and Charlie going away for the day.

Johnson blew out a long breath. "Well, that's a whole heck of a lot to take in."

"Why are you not bothered about the me and Charlie part?" Josh was curious as to why he'd had minimal response to that.

Johnson looked at him for a full minute before answering. "I know someone who has been in a very similar situation. I can't say who, obviously, but it's not as uncommon as many people think."

"How did it work out for them?" Josh would love to know how they managed to make it work. He and Charlie had a lot of hills to climb but as long as they can do it together, he'd be happy. Of course, he needed to make sure Charlie was on the same page first though.

Johnson rolled his lips in. "It didn't." He looked at Josh. "I wish I could give you a better outcome. But for them, it didn't work. The pressure was too much for one of them to bear and they are now living on opposite sides of the country, hardly talking."

Josh deflated a little. It was not what he wanted to hear. He sighed. "Okay, thanks for sharing."

"Can I ask you a personal question, Josh?"

"Yes."

"Do you love him?"

Josh gathered his thoughts for a moment, not quite comfortable telling this to Johnson. "I feel lost without him here. Kind of like I'm hanging on, waiting for my life to mean something again. When I think about him, my heart beats so fast, and I want to smile. When I hear his voice, I'm the same. I hate what he's being put through, and I want to help him feel better about himself."

Johnson laughed. "You could have just said yes."

Josh stared at him, then chuckled. "I didn't realise that's what it was until it all came out, to be honest. Yes, I love him."

"My best advice, on that front, is to make sure you talk. Regardless of how uncomfortable either of you might be or regardless of whether you think he's ready to hear it, you need to talk about it. It's the one thing that went wrong in this other relationship. They could have weathered their way through the comments, stares and anything else if they had realised they were both hanging on by their fingertips."

Josh thought about it and realised it made sense. "Thanks, I will talk to him as soon as I figure out what's going on."

"The sooner the better. As for your situation, I will speak with the college and see what they've got going on so far. Charlie could easily get Jimmy arrested for it, but it's up to him. There is a small chance he wouldn't be convicted, but that picture is worth a thousand words. Whether it's good words or bad words, I don't know. I'll try to dig some information up about Aiden and Travis. I don't recognise either of their names, but I will see what I can find."

Josh stood. "Thanks, man, I really appreciate it."

"No problem. I'll be in touch."

They walked back to the bar, Johnson clapping him on the shoulder as he went back to his friends. Josh realised he'd been gone longer than fifteen minutes. "Sorry, Analise. I didn't expect it to take so long."

"No problem." She cocked her head and looked at him. "Everything okay?" she asked quietly.

"Not yet, but hopefully it will be."

Josh finished working at eleven-thirty. He got into his car when he heard a crack against the window. Turning around in his seat, he saw what looked to be a broken egg on the rear passenger window. He saw and heard another hit, so opened his car door, ducking when another was aimed at his head.

"Scumbag! Freak!"

Josh saw two guys lob more eggs towards him, then run off in the opposite direction. He sighed. He supposed this was something he had to get used to. The conversation with Johnson came to mind. This was probably one of the things he was dancing around. Well, there was nothing he could do at the moment, so he got in his car again and drove home. He would clean the car tomorrow.

17

Charlie

Charlie woke the next morning needing to speak to Josh.

"Hello?" came the groggy reply.

"Josh?"

"Charlie? What time is it?"

Charlie folded the pillow under his head and smiled. "Eight."

"Everything okay?" He cleared his throat, probably to clear his croaky voice.

"Yeah, I was wondering how the conversation with Mum and Dad went yesterday. I thought you'd ring me yesterday and tell me."

"God, sorry, Charlie. After I spoke to them, we had dinner then I went straight to Crush. By the time I'd finished there, it was late, and I didn't want to wake you. I should have messaged you though, sorry."

"It's okay. How did it go?" Charlie was insistent when he needed to know something.

"It went okay. I didn't tell them about what Jimmy did or about the photo, but I did tell them about the other three and everything else. They were a little worried about it, but Dad told me to speak to Johnson. I managed to have a chat with him last night at the bar. He said he was going to look into it for us, see if he can find out any more information."

"That's good of him. Does he know?" He wasn't sure whether he wanted to know or not.

"Yes, I told him. He didn't blink an eye. He knew another couple who'd gone through a similar situation. He wasn't bothered at all."

Charlie released a breath. He was about to say something when he heard his dad's voice on the other end of the line.

"What the hell happened to your car?"

"Good morning, Dad!" Josh replied.

"Tell me."

"Just some hooligans last night. It's nothing to worry about." Josh's voice was neutral, which pricked Charlie's instincts, but he didn't say anything.

"That's okay then. Sorry to barge in."

"Josh, what's going on?" Charlie sounded a little worried, understandably.

"It's nothing. Just some kids playing up. Anyway, how're things over there?"

"It's good. I think I'm okay to head back today. I'm missing the bar."

"Nice to see I'm on the list of what you're missing," Josh teased.

"You know what I mean." Charlie rolled his eyes. "Anyway, I'll let you get back to your sleep."

"No chance of that now. Thanks!"

"Shut up! At least now you're up, you can go for your morning run, can't you? See I helped!" He shook his head.

"Yeah, yeah, whatever helps you sleep at night."

"Shut up, buttbrain. I'm going. Speak to you later. Love you. Bye!"

Charlie clicked to turn off the call, dropped it to the bed and put his head in his hands. Oh God, what had he done? He hadn't meant to say it, but it'd just come out. What was Josh thinking now? Was he upset? Shit! There was no way Charlie could talk to him later now. "What's the saying? That everything comes in threes? Yeah, no shit!" he mumbled to himself.

Cheeks burning in embarrassment, he walked over to the kettle to get some coffee. He was getting antsy not having anything to do. He couldn't remember the last time he'd been so free of obligations. It was unnerving.

He felt his cheeks get warm when he remembered what he'd said. He decided to ring Ginny, speaking as soon as she answered. "I just ended a call with Josh by saying 'love you'! I didn't mean for it to come out, it just did! What is he going to think?" Charlie was getting himself worked up again and tried to breathe slowly to calm his heart.

"Charlie? What time is it? Never mind." He heard Ginny cough, then her voice coming out louder than before. He realised he must have woken her. "I'm sure he's fine about it. If I know Josh, he's probably been waiting for you to say something before he did. You know he'd never want you to feel cornered, so he's probably kept quiet about his feelings."

"I don't know, Gin. Am I in love with him for real? Or am I interested in what I shouldn't have?" Charlie voiced his concerns quietly. "I'm worried we're doing all this because it's not right and not because we care for each other. Oh god, I'm not explaining myself properly." Charlie shook his head in exasperation.

"Okay, listen to me." He heard some noises on the other end, then her voice again. "Answer these questions for me. How do you feel when you think about walking down the street holding Josh's hand?"

"God, I couldn't do that to him! Think of what would be said to us. Everyone we meet would either say something horrible or ignore us. I couldn't do that to Josh."

"Alright, second question. How do you feel when you're in your house together?"

Charlie smiled. "Happy. I love that I can be myself with him. I don't have to pretend to be anything else."

"I think you have your answer then."

Charlie cocked his head in confusion, trying to figure out her response. Ginny sighed. "I can tell by your silence that you don't understand. You don't want anyone hating Josh for your relationship; therefore, would be willing to pretend it wasn't true in public. But at home, you said so yourself, you're happy and free from burdens. That to me, says you're not in this because it's taboo. You're in love with him."

Charlie looked at his face in the mirror opposite him, eyes widening. His hand covered his mouth as he said, "Holy hell."

Ginny laughed. "Yup."

They were silent for a few minutes, while Charlie absorbed the information.

"Thanks for everything. You're amazing."

"Yeah, I know. I'm the best."

Charlie laughed. "Yes, you are."

· • • ● ⬤ • ● ● • • ·

"Hello?"

Josh rushed into the hallway and ploughed into Charlie.

"Umph!" Charlie dropped his bag with a thump, then slid his arms around Josh's waist, one reaching up to rub his back. "Hi, J," he whispered.

Josh didn't say anything. Charlie hadn't realised exactly how much he had missed him until he'd come back through the door. The same for Josh if how tight he was holding him was anything to go by. Josh squeezed him tighter. A throat cleared but they ignored it. Josh burrowed his face into Charlie's neck. "I love you," he whispered so quictly, Charlie wasn't sure if he'd heard right.

Charlie's body started shaking. Josh pulled back a little to look at him, and Charlie realised he was crying. Josh cupped his cheeks, wiping the tears with his fingers. "Is that okay?"

Charlie nodded as more tears fell.

"Why have you made my boy cry?" Josh got pushed aside as their mum took his place, pulling Charlie into a hug. "Are you okay, sweetheart? What did he say to upset you?" His mum looked at Josh, eyes narrowed. "You better have a good explanation, young man."

Josh straightened, looked her in the eye and said, "I told him I loved him."

There was a beat of silence then his mum burst into tears, hugging them both tight, mumbling words he couldn't understand. He was hoping they were happy tears too. But he wasn't sure.

His mum pulled away after a minute and pulled them into the living room. She pushed them both down onto the sofa and she sat on the coffee table facing them. She looked at Josh. "You love him?"

Josh nodded. "With everything I am." He wrapped his arm around Charlie's shoulder.

His mum looked at Charlie. "What about you?"

Charlie nodded. "I love him." Then he turned to Josh, "I love you." A lone tear dripped down his cheek, which Josh wiped away.

His mum clasped her hands to her mouth and laughed. "I'm so happy for you both." She looked at them tenderly for a moment, then her face became serious. "You're going to have many problems, my beautiful boys. There will be people out there," she pointed out the window, "who will try to bring you down with their hate. You must stay strong. Believe in each other. Your dad and I will always be here, no matter what. Friends and family? Don't worry about them," she waved her hand. "If they can't accept you as you are, then you don't need them. Love is unconditional. You remember to believe in each other. Others will try to bend your words, your love, your belief to better suit themselves. If you stay true to yourself—and each other—you will be strong and come out the other side. Make sure you keep talking to each other. Once you stop, it's the first step to a broken relationship."

Josh and Charlie nodded to their mother. "Thank you for your blessing, Mum."

"You have mine too." Their dad came in the room, tears in his eyes. "I know your mother said I did, but I wanted you to hear it from me. You need anything at all, we are here, always and forever."

Charlie burst into tears again and stood up to embrace his father. Josh hugged their mother, thanking her over and over again as she held him. Then they swapped parents and hugged again.

18

Josh

After everything had calmed down a little, Josh and Charlie retreated to his room. They'd had a quick, awkward conversation with their parents about sleeping arrangements and had agreed they were allowed to share a room, but their parents would prefer them not to sleep together yet. Josh thought they wanted them to take things slow, especially with everything that had happened as well as all the things they didn't yet know about.

Josh led Charlie to his bed and laid down, tucking Charlie into his side. He kissed Charlie's head, whispering, "I love you." It felt so surreal. He knew he loved Charlie but had never imagined he would be able to have him.

"I love you, too, J." Charlie whispered back. Before Josh knew it, Charlie had fallen asleep. Setting the alarm on his phone for a couple of hours, he nestled in and fell asleep too.

Josh stirred slowly, realising he was spooned against Charlie like last time. He had his arms around him and tightened them briefly, then let go. Trying not to wake him, Josh rolled to his back then sat up. Grabbing his phone, he realised he'd only slept for an hour, so turned off the alarm; Charlie could sleep as long as he wanted. Josh had to go to the bar tonight.

He walked down the stairs slowly, enjoying the realisation he didn't have to hide here. At home, he was safe and loved, regardless of the situation. It was the outside world that would have the problem, and he wasn't quite sure how they would react to whatever was thrown at them.

"That's a very serious face, son?" His dad was in the kitchen when he entered.

"I was thinking of the outside world and what it means for us."

"It's not going to be easy. Just take it one step at a time. Find out who your real friends are first. That will make it easier."

"Yeah. To do that though, I have to tell people." That sounded bad, so he continued quickly in case his dad got the wrong impression, "Which I want to do anyway. I just know it's going to be hard for Charlie."

"It will be. But you'll be there to support him, as will your mother and me. Did you speak to Johnson, by the way?"

"Yeah, I did. He said he'd contact the college and look into it at his end too. I'm waiting to hear back from him or the college."

· · · ● · ● ● · ● · ●

Josh headed out to Crush, leaving a note on the bedside table for Charlie when he woke. He looked exhausted, even in sleep, which made Josh think he'd not slept much while he'd been away.

Entering the bar, he headed straight for the office, hoping Tom would be in. He wasn't in the office, but Josh found him talking with two guys in the outdoor area. Not wanting to interrupt, he turned to walk away, but Tom called him over.

"Josh, this is Sean and Max." Tom indicated each of the men as he said their names. "The owner wants to create a better used outdoor space, so they're here to see what can be done with what's available. I was thinking of making it a quiet, soothing area, more comfortable chairs and tables with lighting for when it gets dark." Josh noticed Tom was gesturing wildly about the prospect.

"We're going to be closing the deck section in a couple of days, boarding the section off to make sure only the contractors and I can come back here until it's finished. Hopefully, the anticipation of what is going on will bring some attention to us, which should lead to customers coming by and spending more money."

Josh was impressed. It sounded amazing, and he could just imagine what it would look like. "If you put some twinkling lights overhead, it would make it more romantic too." Josh had a thought that he could bring Charlie out here one day.

"Good idea," said Max, nodding while looking around.

"If we use the vines that are thriving already," Sean added, "and twine them around an arbour, we can add some potted plants and other vines to enclose the area more. That way, people will feel more sheltered, but the view of the river will still be spread out in front of them. We won't stop anything from blocking that view." Sean seemed as enthusiastic as the rest.

"Seems like we have a plan, gentlemen. Can you work it all up for me to have a look at then I'll speak with the owner?" Tom asked, gesturing them back inside.

"Of course." They shook hands. "We'll be in touch soon. Nice to meet you, Josh," Sean said.

"Yeah, you too."

Tom and Josh continued to the office. "Did you need to see me for some reason?" Tom asked him as they entered.

Josh closed the door behind him then brought Tom up to speed, confirming Charlie and he were beginning a relationship then asked a question he'd been worried about.

"I wanted to ask." He bit his lip, nervous. "How do you want us to behave when we're in the bar together?"

Tom looked at Josh, then down to his desk. "Um, I'd not really thought about it."

"I'm happy to do whatever you'd like. I was a little concerned if we kissed or something, people in the bar would stop coming.

I don't want it to hurt your business. So, you tell me what you want, and we'll be fine with it."

Tom was quiet for a moment. He stood from his chair with a sigh. "How did you know it was my business? I've kept that quiet for years."

Josh shrugged. "You can do every job here. You always do the paperwork. You hire the staff. I've never seen or heard from the owner. It made sense. But I didn't know for definite until you confirmed."

Tom laughed. "Okay, hotshot, keep quiet then will you. I don't want the staff treating me different because I own the place. That was the reason I kept it quiet in the first place."

Josh nodded in understanding. "No problem."

"As for your question, treat each other as you would if you were in a normal relationship. If you want to kiss him, do it. If the customers can't bear it, then I don't want them here. This will be a sanctuary for you to be whoever you want to be."

Josh burst into tears, feeling himself being folded into Tom's arms. Dad was right when he said Josh would feel better once he knew who he could rely on. Pulling back, he said, wetly, "Thank you. You don't know how much that means to me. To us."

Tom gestured to the bathroom. "Get yourself cleaned up and come out when you're ready."

Josh did as he was told, giving himself a few more minutes to calm his red face. Crying always made him a blotchy mess. Sniffing, he exited the office and went to the counter to start his training. Tom was showing him some things tonight, at least for an hour or so until Rob came in.

A couple of hours later, Charlie showed up on the wrong side of the bar. "Hey, bartender! Can I get a drink?" Josh looked up, a smile blossoming on his face.

He moved over to him and leaned forward. He whispered to Charlie, "Can I kiss you?" watching his face to see his reaction. "Tom is alright with it if you are."

Charlie looked around the bar at the customers in residence. He bit his lip.

"Oh, Charlie. Just kiss him already." Analise bumped Josh on the shoulder while looking Charlie in the eyes. "We're all good."

Charlie smiled, then looked at Josh. "I'm worried about the reaction of everyone. I don't know if I could stand for everyone to make comments."

Josh pulled back, understanding this was hard for Charlie. "Okay, no sweat. We'll wait." He poured Charlie a beer, putting it in front of him, proudly showing off his new skills.

"Not bad, for a beginner. We'll have you in the Olympics yet."

Josh frowned. "There is an Olympic sport for bartending?"

Charlie and Analise burst out laughing. Once they'd calmed down enough to talk, they explained about a small competition some bartenders enter called National Cocktail competition. They explained there were other competitions out there, but it was not an Olympic sport. Yet.

Another couple of hours went by with Josh immersed in drinks, service and conversation. It was weird being on the wrong side of the bar, but it also made Josh happy they could share this.

Josh grabbed the full bag of rubbish and took it to the bin in the alley before coming back to the bar. As he returned, he saw Charlie and Analise deep in conversation. Charlie noticed him, sat up straighter, then slipped off the stool.

Looking towards Analise, he saw her smiling as she watched Charlie's progress towards him. Josh waited at the entrance to the bar, bemused.

"Everything okay?" was all he managed to get out before Charlie's lips slammed down on his own. His own arms went around Charlie's waist while Charlie wrapped his around Josh's neck. He nipped at Charlie's mouth, requesting entry then swooped in. They feasted on each other for a few long minutes before some background noise filtered into Josh's ears. He broke away slowly, not wanting to break their connection. They were panting into each other's mouth.

Finally, the noise in the bar returned full force and Josh reluctantly let Charlie go but kept his arms around his waist. The bar wasn't as loud as before and as Josh looked around, he saw nearly everyone staring at them. Some faces looked disgusted, some were curious, others were downright glaring in hatred. Amazingly though, some were smiling.

Josh turned to the bar to see Analise smiling, Rob glaring and Tom stood on top of the bar.

"—and if you don't like what you've seen then you are welcome to leave. This bar will forever be a welcoming one. We welcome anyone except people who will make trouble. I can see several of you I will be asking to leave and not return if you don't leave of your own volition. Charlie and Josh have found something most of us only dream of. Leave them be." Tom jumped down to a small amount of clapping. He turned to Rob, taking the cloth off him. "You can leave, Rob." Josh heard Charlie gasp, then he clung tighter as Rob glared at them, turned and left.

"Oh God, I'm so sorry, Tom. I didn't think about the repercussions." Charlie started rambling away before Tom held up a hand.

"I've already spoken to Josh about this, and it's absolutely fine. You're welcome here more than anyone else. Don't hide away. Customers who have open views will always be welcome. Everyone else can go to hell. Including staff." Tom added as he looked at the door Rob just went through. "Come on, get back to work." He chuckled. "Charlie, do you fancy finishing Rob's shift?"

Charlie smiled in happiness. "Of course, I will."

Josh pecked Charlie on the lips, then swooped his arm in front of him allowing Charlie entry first. The rest of the shift went by without issue, even if there were still a few lingering stares, nothing was said to them.

· · · ● · ● · ● · · ·

The next morning, Josh received a phone call from Mr Reynolds, asking him to come into the office for a chat. He wouldn't explain what it was about over the phone, so Josh was left to wonder until he got there.

Mr Reynolds opened the door at his knock, allowing him entry before closing it again.

"Good morning, Josh, thank you for coming in." Mr Reynolds moved around to sit at his desk, indicating the empty seat in front of it. "I have some news regarding the investigation into those photos."

Josh sat down in the chair and waited for him to continue.

"We received a visit from Mr Carter, who said he was representing you from a legal standpoint. He was very insistent everything was handed over to him, which we have done. We were able to locate the original email source. It came from Aiden White. I understand you had a relationship with him."

"Yes, we were in a relationship for about a year, until I caught him cheating on me. We broke up last week."

"Yes, well, the police have now been informed as the photos were deemed to be shared without consent. The police will be here shortly to take your statement."

"If that's the case, I need to make two short phone calls," Josh said, quickly retrieving his phone from his pocket.

Mr Reynolds indicated he could. Josh decided to stay where he was. Dialling Johnson's number, he quickly explained the situation, and Johnson told him he'd be there shortly. Dialling Charlie's number next, he started talking when he answered. "Hey, I'm at college. They've found who leaked the photos and the police have been called. I think you need to come down here and speak to them too." He paused.

"Do you think it's a good idea?" Charlie asked.

"Yes, I do, Charlie. Come down here, I'll wait in the office for you. You won't be alone. You can always call Ginny if you want her instead."

Charlie was quiet for a moment. "Okay, I'll see you in a bit."

"Okay, love you, bye."

"Love you, too. Bye." Josh ended the call, looking at Mr Reynolds. He had his fingers steepled in front of his mouth, eyes narrowed. "Yes, Mr Reynolds, we are in a relationship. But I'm assured, by my solicitor, it will not be an issue. Is that correct?" Josh was pushing, but he needed to know.

"Absolutely, no issue at all, Josh." Mr Reynolds cleared his throat. "Aiden has already been detained by the police, so you won't need to be worried at present about running into him. He has been taken out of the college and won't be returning. The photos have been deleted as much as possible, but Mr Carter said he would be using his legal means to remove the rest of them."

Josh blew out a breath. "Thank God."

"This means, once you have spoken with the police, and I'm assuming Charlie will be speaking with them, too, you are free to return to your classes as soon as you wish."

"Thank you, sir. I may need a day or two, but I will return."

"Take what you need." The intercom on his desk phone buzzed, and he picked up the receiver. "Send them in." He replaced the phone, looking to Josh. "The police have arrived. I will take you to a spare office, so you have a confidential space to talk in." He paused. "You have my word I will not say anything about your relationship."

There was a knock at the door, and it opened revealing two police offices and Johnson.

"Follow me." They walked a couple of doors down. "I will leave you to your conversation. I shall let you know when Charlie arrives, Josh."

"Thank you, Mr Reynolds."

• • • ● ● • ● ● • • •

Josh blew out a breath. He was exhausted. He'd been speaking with the police officers, Detective Sergeant Logan Taylor and Police Constable Ava Walker, for over an hour. About forty minutes in, he'd been told Charlie and Ginny had arrived, but the police continued to talk to Josh. He'd been through everything, making sure to include comments about Charlie's adoption, in case anything came out. Johnson was there through it all which helped.

He left the office with Johnson, seeing Charlie as soon as he'd exited. He gave him a hug, quietly telling him the police didn't know about their relationship, for obvious reasons, and telling him to remember to tell them he was adopted. After another brief hug, he let go.

"Everything is going to be fine, Charlie. I'll be there the whole time. I'll stop them if I have to," Johnson said.

"Do you want one of us to come in with you?" Ginny asked Charlie. She looked at Johnson. "Is that okay?" He nodded.

Charlie nodded. He looked at Josh. "Would you mind if Ginny came? It's not that I don't want—"

"Charlie, it's fine. I know it's a difficult subject to talk about. It's not a problem at all. I'll be here when you come out."

Charlie nodded again. "Thanks, J."

They entered the office, closing the door, and Josh sank into a chair outside. He could understand why Charlie didn't want him in there. He was sure there was information which would anger him, and he was probably better not knowing. He was there for a lot longer than two hours and, when the door finally opened, Charlie rushed into his arms, holding him tight. Josh noticed Ginny looked wrecked. The police officers and Johnson followed them shortly after, eyes on Charlie and Josh.

Josh reluctantly separated from Charlie but kept his arm around him.

"Now, we will do our investigation with help from Mr Carter, and we'll be in touch." Josh shook the police officers' hands, and then they were on their way. He blew out another breath.

"They don't know anything about your relationship, except suspicions, but even if they did, you'd be fine. Charlie's adoption is registered legally, so you are able to have a relationship without a fallback. If you were full siblings, they'd be a problem, but adopted, you're good." Johnson explained.

"Thank God!" said Ginny.

"The police already have Aiden in custody, and from what they implied, he's squealed on Jimmy already. They are looking out for him now. As for Travis, they are picking him up because they had a complaint of harassment lodged by Tom." Josh's eyebrows rose. "Yes, I told him to." Johnson smiled. "It's all interlinked. We needed everything in place. Now, I'm going to let you get home and rest up. I will be in touch later today with more information." Johnson waved goodbye and was gone.

"He's awesome!" said Ginny.

"Yeah, not sure what we'd have done without him," Josh said.

They all went their separate ways outside of college. Ginny went to see Tom, and Josh took Charlie home.

As they pulled in the driveway, they saw their Dad washing his car. He stopped to watch them get out then threw the sponge back in the bucket when he saw the state Charlie was in.

"What's happened?"

"We have something to talk to you about." Josh and Charlie had spoken briefly on the drive deciding now the police were involved, they had to explain everything to their parents.

"Okay, let's get you inside then." Dad rushed into the house, calling for their Mum.

Sitting down and talking to them was difficult, especially as Charlie refused to divulge some of the information. They all got the idea though.

Mum sobbed during the retelling, Dad reaching around her to keep her close. Afterwards, they sat and drank some tea.

Josh's phone rang, startling them all. He saw it was Johnson, so put it on speaker.

"Hey, Johnson. You're on speaker with Charlie, Mum and Dad."

"Hi, Josh. Hi, everyone. Good news. The police have found Jimmy and Travis already, and everyone is now behind bars for the moment."

"Great news, thanks."

"What happens now?" Dad asked.

"Well, we have to wait for the police to do their part of the investigation, but it shouldn't take them too long. They have everything found by me and the college, plus they seized every-one's phones. There is a lot of evidence piling up against them. I will keep hounding them as much as I can, and I'll let you know as soon as I know more."

"Thank you, Johnson. It's much appreciated."

Josh hung up the phone and looked at Charlie. "You did good, Charlie Bear." Charlie turned towards him and curled into his arms. Josh was so happy they could relax here. It would make things a little easier on them. But he decided it would be better to start getting used to what was happening in the outside world, so he suggested meeting Ginny and Tom for lunch. Charlie readily agreed and got on the phone with Ginny to arrange it.

Half an hour later, they were on their way to Pop's. Josh knew this was probably a bad idea because everyone knew everyone in Pop's. He wasn't sure what the reception was going to be like, but they had to face it at some point. When he parked the car, he turned to Charlie and asked him if he was okay.

"Yeah, a little nervous. We're not in our little bubble anymore. I have to say I'm worried about what people are going to say or do." Charlie shivered and rubbed his arms.

"I know. I'm not sure either. But it's better to know now than hide away, isn't it?" Josh talked the talk, but if Charlie insisted on leaving, Josh would be out of there quicker than ever. "Come on, we're together, let's act it and let what happens happen."

Charlie blew out a breath, then took a deep one in again. "Let's go." They both opened their doors and got out. Charlie circled the car to Josh's side and grabbed his hand in a tight grip. Giving him a small smile and a hand squeeze, they walked towards the entrance.

The bell jingled as they went in, making heads turn in their direction. There was a considerable drop in conversation as they made their way to the table Ginny and Tom were already sitting at. Josh motioned Charlie to go into the booth seat first, then he slid in.

"Hey, guys!" piped up Ginny, trying, fairly successfully, to act like this was normal. Not the having lunch together—that was normal. It was the having eyes on them constantly that was new.

"Hi." Charlie ducked his head, using his finger to draw lines on the table.

The waitress arrived, showing barely concealed disgust and asked for their order. Each of them ordered a meal and a drink, watching as she slunk away.

"Who wants to bet we get spit in our food?" Josh laughed, trying to lighten the mood. Ginny and Tom laughed with him, and Charlie made a small smile.

As they waited for the food and drink, Josh got them caught up with the information Johnson had told them about the case. "We're waiting for him to update us more." At that, the waitress returned, almost throwing the drinks on the table before skulking off again. Man, it was going to get old.

"Have you heard from anyone else?" Ginny asked.

Charlie shook his head, so did Josh. "No. No one has been in contact at all. Friends or enemies. I guess Dad was right when he said we'd know who our friends were when the time came." Josh shook his head, turning his head when a couple of guys walked past their table.

"Brother-fuckers!" they said, quietly enough not to be heard by too many people, then sniggered, bumping each other's shoulders as if they'd made a huge job.

"I have to admit that was a fairly good one," Josh said, nodding his head. "They might have a career in stand-up comedy." He jumped when a plate was slammed down in front of him, nearly spilling the contents. "Do you mind?" he asked the waitress.

"Yes, I mind a lot as a matter of fact," she responded.

"Donna! Leave them alone!" Pop came out from the back kitchen with Maria following behind.

"But—"

"But nothing. They are customers who have come here to eat. Now leave them be." Donna huffed and walked away while Pop came closer. Everyone in the whole town called him Pop. Josh didn't even know what his real name was. It didn't matter though, young or old, Pop is what they called him. Maria was his daughter. "I'm sorry about that, young Charlie and Josh. I've no excuse for her, but I'll make sure she doesn't serve you in future if that is her stance." Pop leaned down on the table and made eye contact with them both. "You are welcome here. Regardless of what others think, you will be welcome here. I cannot guarantee the environment will always be friendly because I cannot control everyone's mouths, as much as I would like to. But never fear coming here. You got that?"

"Yes, Pop."

"Thanks, Pop."

He nodded his head. "Maria will serve you from now on." He tapped their table and headed back to his kitchen.

Maria smiled at them, asking if they needed anything.

"No, we're all good for the moment, thanks."

"No problem, wave me over if you do." She walked off back to the counter.

There was the odd comment and several customers staring at them, but for the most part, they were left alone. When they'd all finished their food, they hung around for one more cup of coffee and then decided to head out. Exiting the café after waving bye to Maria, they saw the two guys from earlier surrounding Josh's car.

Josh wasn't stupid. He knew if he went over there, there'd be trouble. So, he called out from where he was, making sure Charlie was behind him, and they were still in view of the café.

"Can I help you?"

The guys turned around to look at them. "Yeah." One of them leered. "We don't tolerate sibling-suckers here. You need to find a new town."

Josh was most impressed by the fact they were able to string alliterated words together, let alone used the word 'tolerate'. "I'm afraid we can't do that. We live here too. Thanks for the advice though." Josh didn't move any closer. He was glad he didn't when the other guy pulled a tyre iron from behind his back. He flinched but didn't move when guy smashed his back window, only reaching his hand behind him to try and bring some comfort to Charlie, who was sobbing against his back.

Pop came rushing out the café, "The police are on their way. Arnie and Derek, you should be ashamed of yourselves! What would your mother think about your behaviour?" He stopped shouting at them after they had run off around the far corner of the car park. Pop turned to them. "It will get easier, boys. Just take it a day at a time. You'll survive. You know where I am if you need anything. Send the police through once you're done talking to them."

Josh heard the sirens and turned to Charlie, enveloping him in his arms. "It's okay, Charlie. I've got you."

It just so happened to be the same officers who came to the college earlier that day.

"Josh, Charlie. Sorry we have to see you again so soon," said Detective Sergeant Taylor.

"Me too." The police proceeded to ask questions and get a statement from them about the incident. Josh relayed the message from Pop, and after checking they were okay to go, led Charlie away from them and over to where Ginny and Tom were waiting.

Ginny pulled Charlie into a hug while Tom rested his hand on Josh's shoulder.

"How're you holding up?" Tom asked him quietly.

Josh looked at him and shrugged. "It's as bad as I was expecting, so nothing too overwhelming. Yet."

"Let's get you both home. Come on, I'll give you a lift."

"Thanks, Tom."

• • • ● • ● ● • • •

Yet again, they had some explaining to do when they got home. Unfortunately, those two police officers were seen more than they wanted to be over the next few weeks. Josh's car was vandalised again after it had been fixed. Charlie's had been spray painted with graffiti. Eggs had been thrown at their home and their faces if they were walking in the street.

Charlie was getting to breaking point, but Josh stayed with him, talking themselves through it like several people had said they needed to. It seemed to centre Charlie after each conversation, so Josh made sure to talk every night before they went to sleep.

They still hadn't slept together. There was too much going on, too many stresses to make it memorable. Josh wanted to wait until the perfect moment, but he wasn't sure when it was going to be.

19

Charlie

The day of the court case came sooner than they were expecting. They had originally been told it would be eight months or more before the cases came to court, but Johnson had managed to get it brought forward so all three of them were charged at the same time. His argument to the judge was the three cases were all intermingled, and it would be better to try it all at the same time. The judge agreed, so today, two months after the original statement with the police, Charlie was standing in front of his mirror getting dressed in his best suit.

He was not at all ready to see Jimmy again, but he supposed this would be the last time, hopefully. Johnson said he had a very good case against him, so Charlie was keeping all his fingers and toes crossed.

He sighed as arms came around his waist, and Josh pressed his cheek to Charlie's.

"Hey, handsome," Josh said with a smile. "Look at you."

Charlie blushed and met Josh's eyes in the mirror. "You should talk, that grey suit looks amazing on you." Charlie turned in his arms and ran his hands down Josh's suit front. "Mmm, you look good in this colour."

Josh pinched his chin between his finger and thumb and gently kissed Charlie on the lips. "How are you doing?"

"I'm okay. I'll be better once this is done. Johnson said it should all be over and done with today? Didn't he?"

"Yes. I'll be there for you. So will Mum, Dad, Ginny, Tom, Maria and Pop. Everyone is here for you."

Charlie smiled and kissed Josh again, a little more persistent this time.

"Boys, it's time to go!"

They both pulled apart laughing. "Do you think she knows when we do that? She always seems to call us when we're kissing!"

Holding hands, they descended the stairs, meeting their parents at the bottom.

"Good, you're both ready. Let's go." His mum was whittling away about the case. She also wasn't very happy with Charlie because he had asked that she not be present when his testimony was read out. He didn't want her to listen to what happened when it wasn't necessary. Charlie couldn't explain what he felt when Johnson had told him he didn't need to go on the witness stand. He had been beyond relieved. He was still going to be in the room at the prosecution table, but Josh would be next to him, as would Johnson.

The drive over was quiet, nobody knowing what to say. His dad parked the car and they all got out for the short walk to the courthouse.

Charlie grabbed Josh's hand as they entered. He was shaking so much, he didn't think his legs would hold him up much longer. His mum and dad pulled them into a hug, then let them go forward while they sat behind them.

Johnson greeted them with handshakes. "Hey, guys. It's nearly done with. Try to relax. Remember you don't need to say anything. And you don't need to look at anyone unless you want to. Have a seat. We'll be starting in about ten minutes."

Charlie sat with Josh, looking down into his lap where he had taken Josh's hand. Suddenly, Josh's other hand covered theirs.

"Charlie, look at me."

He looked.

"We are going to be fine. Relax for me." Josh kept eye contact as he breathed, and Charlie noticed he was changing his breathing to match.

"Thanks."

"All rise!" The voice of the usher made Charlie's heart begin to gallop again. He stood, still holding onto Josh's hand like a lifeline. The judge came in and sat on her bench, then they all sat down.

As the proceedings began, Charlie heard Jimmy, Aiden and Travis being led into the room. He kept looking forward, refusing to look at them. Josh squeezed his hand in support.

The charges for each were read out. Charlie had been warned that the defence would make it look like he had consented to the photos with Jimmy, but he didn't have to say anything in his defence; his statement was being read out for him.

When the proceedings started on the case against Jimmy, Charlie felt his throat dry up. He kept his eyes on his lap, face burning with humiliation as his statement was read, detailing what had happened. He felt his tears begin to roll down his cheeks. Josh's hand squeezed tightly around his as the reading came to the part about Jimmy pulling his trousers down and Charlie could feel Josh's banked fury. Charlie squeezed back, just as tightly.

The defence tried to say that Charlie had consented to having sex with Jimmy and, when Jimmy found out Charlie was a virgin and said he couldn't do it, Charlie had turned around and decided to make Jimmy pay for it. It was as bad as Johnson had predicted, but Charlie was mortified that they had brought his virginity into it.

Johnson argued that the photo did not make sense if it had happened the way the defence described. He explained that Charlie's facial expression did not show anger or pleasure, which, if Jimmy's testimony was true, it should have done.

The back and forth of the debate was mind-blowing, and Charlie tuned out for some of it because he didn't understand the legal terms they used.

The judge eventually had heard enough about Jimmy's case and turned to Aiden's. Johnson showed the evidence to prove that the original photos had been sent from Aiden's phone. Defence questioned the legitimacy of that information but was shot down. Josh's statement was read out regarding his interactions with Aiden. Johnson also presented a statement from Kent, which they had not known about. It put Aiden's monogamous claims in the toilet. Charlie allowed a small smile at that. Kent had provided the names of all the people he knew Aiden had been with, then Johnson proved those claims with first-hand statements from the other guys.

Aiden's name was dragged through the mud with everything he had done to try and get Josh to stay with him. The reason for it became clear when the court was told Aiden's father had told Aiden he would not get university paid for unless he could prove his outlandish ways had improved. Charlie snorted. That didn't work.

Then the court began on Travis's case. It was minor in relation to the other two, but he had still been harassing Tom with phone calls and emails for a three-month period. The phone calls alone totalled over two hundred. The emails were just as numerous. Travis had been dragged into Aiden's plan because, in Aiden's warped mind, he thought by getting Travis in place at the bar, Josh would be more inclined to go there and become a family member.

Charlie didn't understand the way Aiden's mind worked because it certainly didn't make much sense to him.

Finally, Johnson detailed the plan the three of them had come up with in all its glory. Jimmy and Aiden had both taken photos of Josh and Charlie in compromising positions, as innocent as they may have been in reality, and Aiden had put them all together to send out as a bulk email. Once that had been done, social media would do the rest. Aiden had hoped Josh would come to him licking his wounds. Travis had wanted the job because he loved working at a bar and had lost his other position, after an affair with the manager. And Jimmy had wanted Josh.

Yeah, that had come out in the conclusion, shocking them all. Jimmy had admitted that he hadn't even wanted Charlie, just wanted to hurt him because of being refused. But Jimmy had wanted Josh at the end of it all. How Jimmy thought that would happen, Charlie didn't know, but apparently, Josh is one of the few people Jimmy had not had the pleasure of sleeping with.

The judge went off to deliberate on her decision, and Charlie sat quietly while Johnson and Josh talked with their parents. His head was too fuzzy; he was trying to keep from passing out. It was only Josh's hand that kept him sitting still.

Before long, Josh tugged him up to a stand, and Charlie realised the judge had returned.

The judge went through her decision, and Charlie couldn't believe it. Jimmy was going to prison for four years. Aiden was going to prison for two years, and Travis has been given a community service order for one year and a restraining order for Tom and Crush. He didn't hear another word after that.

He got pulled to standing again once the judge left, and then Josh pulled him into his arms. Charlie tucked his head into Josh's neck and breathed.

"Is he okay?" Johnson asked.

Josh answered for him. "Yeah, a little out of it."

"Charlie?" Johnson tried to get his attention. Charlie lifted his head and looked at Johnson. "You did it. Are you okay?"

Charlie took a breath and nodded.

Charlie gave a small smile, then leant against Josh and sobbed. It was over.

• • • ● • ● ● • • •

After they got home, Josh collected a couple of bags which had been packed and had ushered Charlie into his car without even a goodbye to his parents. Driving off hurriedly, Charlie laughed.

"What has gotten into you? Where are we going?"

"To a hotel for the night."

"What! Why?"

"Ginny and Tom have bought a room for the night as a gift for getting through the court case. That's where we're heading."

"Okay." Charlie frowned. "But why?" He didn't understand why they couldn't relax at home. At least he didn't understand until Josh gave him a look. "Oh!" At that, he couldn't contain his grin. We can do anything you want or we can quite easily stay and order loads of room service and binge watch TV."

Charlie rested his head on the headrest and rolled to face Josh. "It's a perfect idea."

For the rest of the journey, they talked about anything and everything. They didn't have anything hanging over their heads at that moment. They were free.

Josh eventually stopped at a nice hotel about an hour away from home. Charlie had fallen asleep for the last part of the journey and had jolted awake when the car had stopped.

"God, sorry. Didn't realise I was so tired." He rubbed his eyes, then his whole face to try and wake himself up.

"It's okay. You probably had about as much sleep as I did last night." Charlie had asked Josh to let him sleep alone last night. He knew he'd be tossing and turning and didn't want to disturb him. But, in hindsight, they probably would have slept better being wrapped around each other.

"Come on, let's check-in." Josh got their bags from the car. Charlie followed behind, staring around at what he could see.

Within a few minutes, they were in the lift going to the tenth floor and then opening their door. Charlie stared in awe at the room they'd been given. There was a huge bed to the side, opposite a desk and minibar, huge wardrobe space and a huge bathroom with shower and bath. But it was the view which caught his attention the most. The window was huge and overlooking the back of the hotel, which was mainly trees and fields as far as he could see. He walked over to it, chucking his suit jacket over the chair as he passed before resting his hand on the windowpane, mesmerised by the picture.

He felt Josh walk up behind him and press him fully against the window. Josh smoothed his hands up Charlie's sides, making Charlie drop his head to the side. Josh took advantage and kissed up his neck to his ear before tugging on the lobe.

"If you don't want to do this, tell me, Charlie. It's not a problem to wait. I love you, regardless."

Charlie sighed. "I love you too. And it's wonderful. I can't wait."

Josh groaned in Charlie's ear, nibbling on his lobe again, before turning him around and kissing him fiercely. They attacked each other's mouths as they had never done before. Being in a house with their parents was not conducive to sexual encounters, though they'd managed a few over the weeks.

Charlie held onto Josh's head to keep himself upright as much as anything else. Josh's hands were everywhere. He felt Josh pull his shirt from his trousers and begin to undo the buttons. Charlie pulled at the collar of Josh's shirt trying to get his point across without the use of his voice. Josh pulled his mouth away only to pull his own shirt over his head and throw it aside before returning to ravage Charlie's mouth again.

Charlie couldn't think. Josh's hands and mouth were sucking all thought from him. All except for the feel of his hands on Josh's skin. He moved his hands continuously over the skin, feeling how warm and hard Josh was.

He broke away for air and slammed his head back against the window as Josh sucked at his neck. Josh had managed to get the buttons undone on Charlie's shirt and pushed it off his shoulders. Charlie didn't want to let go of Josh to get rid of it, but at Josh's chuckle, he let go one hand at a time.

When he was free of his shirt, Josh put his arms around Charlie and pulled him close, skin to skin. Charlie let out a sigh of relief. Skin to skin with Josh was his favourite. Josh kissed him, slowly this time, allowing their lips to sip and taste, and their tongues to explore their mouths. It made Charlie light-headed. The feel of Josh's mouth on his, his fingers on Charlie's back and sides, and Charlie's hands on Josh was so much sensation, Charlie felt like a live wire.

Then he felt Josh moving him along as they danced about the room—at least it felt like they were dancing. Charlie knew he was safe with Josh, so let him lead wherever he wanted him to go. A nudge at the back of his legs informed him he was beside the bed. Josh cupped the back of Charlie's head and lower back and gently laid him on the bed, covering him with his own body as they went.

They continued to kiss until breathing became almost impossible. Josh pulled away slowly, pecking at Charlie's lips, even as he was panting hard.

Looking into Charlie's eyes, he said, "I love you, Charlie."

Tears pooled in his eyes. Trying to breathe through his emotions, Charlie replied, "I love you, too." Josh sank into him, resting his head in Charlie's neck. He was heavy, but Charlie loved the feel of him like this. It made him feel wanted. And loved. Even though the words had been said many times, it was the way Josh made him feel that mattered more.

Josh began to torture Charlie with kisses along his neck and down his collarbone.

"Mmm." Charlie liked the feel of it and ran his hands through Josh's hair. Josh was licking and nipping at his skin as he worked his way down his stomach. He flicked the button on Charlie's trousers open and unzipped slowly. Charlie looked at Josh, seeing his eyes on his. Josh smiled and kissed his lower abdomen, above his boxers.

"Fuck, Charlie, you taste amazing. I can't get enough." Josh pulled Charlie's trousers down his legs and threw them behind him, his socks following quickly after.

Charlie used his feet to propel himself back onto the bed more fully. Josh followed, kissing his lips again, more passionately that time. Charlie was losing his breath again; he couldn't get enough of Josh's mouth. Getting side-tracked by Charlie's nipples, Josh began his torment. Charlie was sensitive there, so it didn't take much to get him writhing on the bed, gasping. "Josh! Ah!" He held Josh's head but wasn't sure if he was pushing him away or pulling him closer. Josh gave the other nipple the same treatment.

Josh rested some of his weight on Charlie's lower body, giving his cock a little friction, making Charlie moan with desire.

"God, Charlie. I love the noises you make." Josh began kissing further down his body until he reached his underwear, while still rubbing his fingers over Charlie's nipples. Looking up at Charlie as if to check he was still on board, Josh used his other hand to grasp his cock through them. He tightened his grip, making a little up and down motion, pulling another groan from Charlie.

Josh grabbed Charlie's boxers and pulled them over his cock, releasing it from its confines. He slid them down Charlie's legs and off to somewhere on the floor. Josh grasped his cock gently in his hand and licked the whole length, ending with a little tease at his nerve-filled underside.

"Shit, Josh!" Charlie's back bowed off the bed in pleasure. Josh laved down his cock again towards his balls, gulping when Josh sucked one into his mouth and rolled his tongue around it. He went on to the other one, giving it the same treatment. After a few moments, Charlie felt Josh move his hand forward and almost jumped off the bed when Josh flicked his taint. "Oh, my fucking god!"

Josh chuckled and moved back to Charlie's cock.

"Oh!" Charlie gasped in pleasure as Josh's mouth engulfed the head without warning. His hips bucked up, wanting more wet heat. Josh took him again and again, building up the pleasure until Charlie was thrashing on the bed, pleading to come. "I'm going to come!" Charlie was very nearly there when Josh pulled off and grabbed the base of Charlie's cock hard. Charlie huffed as his orgasm receded some. "Josh, that was not nice!" he panted, although couldn't quite manage an angry tone.

"Sorry, but you'll get there soon."

Getting off the bed, Josh quickly undressed, grabbed the lube from his bag and joined Charlie back on the bed again. They'd had the condom conversation and had both been tested negative since.

Josh laid himself over Charlie, making him open his legs to create room for him. Their cocks came into contact, and both hissed in pleasure. Josh bracketed Charlie's face with his hands and kissed him gently, softly moving his lower body to create a small amount of friction. This was the furthest they had been before. They had come this way a couple of times, but Charlie knew this was just the beginning.

"You ready?" Josh asked him. Charlie nodded, eager for more.

Josh released him and worked his way down again, taking the lube with him.

"Spread your legs more Charlie, let me see you." Charlie pulled his legs as far back as he could, feeling his face grow hot with embarrassment. "Oh, you're gorgeous." Josh licked a stripe up Charlie's cock while he put lube on his fingers. Flicking his tongue against Charlie's sensitive nerves repeatedly, Josh circled a lubed finger around Charlie's hole. He rubbed his finger around his hole, pressing harder on each passing.

"Oh God, Josh." Charlie threw his head back against the bed. He didn't know if he'd survive this. He felt Josh push at him, and Charlie bore down as Josh had explained to do. As the tip of his finger penetrated, Charlie felt a slight sting and hissed. Josh stopped moving.

"It's okay, Charlie. Give me a minute, and it will feel better." Josh engulfed his cock again, trying to keep him hard and distracted as he worked his finger further into his ass. It was slow going, and Charlie had to breathe deeply several times, but they got there. Josh lapped at Charlie's cock as he slowly withdrew his finger until only the tip was in and then moved back in again. It still hurt, but it wasn't as painful as that first time. Each penetration was less pain and more pleasure, especially with Josh licking at his cock head.

Charlie felt himself relax.

"Well done, Charlie. That's it. Relax for me." Josh crooned to him as he kept going with one finger. "It may sting a little more, Charlie. I'm going to try another finger."

Charlie tried to keep his body as relaxed as it was, but he did clench a little as Josh entered a second finger. Again, Josh began lapping at his head and slit, making Charlie dizzy with delight as the pleasure flowed through him. He barely realises Josh has both fingers inside him until a spike of bliss coursed through him.

"Oh, my! Fuck! Josh!" The pleasure of his prostate and nerves being assailed made him seconds from coming. Josh eased him back off the edge again by working a third finger in his ass. By this point, Charlie only felt a very slight flare of pain before the pleasure was overriding it.

Charlie had no idea what he was saying to Josh. He had been unaware of how high this would take him. Josh was about average size-wise he thought, but he knew he would seem bigger.

Josh went slowly, gently pushing a fourth finger in when it was time. Charlie's babbling got louder with the occasional coherent curse thrown in. When Charlie was taking his four fingers easily, Josh released his cock. Charlie looked at Josh, eyes glazed.

"I want you. Now!"

Josh chuckled and knelt between Charlie's legs while he slicked his cock with lube. He wrapped a hand around both of their cocks as he leaned down to kiss Charlie. His mouth opened for his tongue immediately, and Charlie grabbed Josh's head, taking his tongue deeper until they were breathing hard again.

Josh pulled away, holding his cock with one hand and resting the other on the bed next to Charlie's head. Charlie stared at Josh as he pushed forward slowly, and Charlie felt a stretch.

"Oh god! Josh! Fuck, fuck, fuck!" Charlie writhed beneath Josh, making him enter him quicker than had been planned. They both hissed as pleasure streaked through him.

"Fuck, Charlie!" Josh pushed in a little more, then withdrew again, going deeper each time until he was completely seated in Charlie's ass. He paused for a moment, but Charlie was having none of it. He was almost delirious.

"Move, damn you! Fuck!" Charlie's back bowed off the bed, hands gripping Josh's straining arms.

Josh lost some control. He pulled back and thrust in over and over again, nailing Charlie's prostate every time. Charlie made garbled noises.

"Fuck. I'm not going to last! Charlie! Come, Charlie!" Josh fell over Charlie, bracing himself on one elbow, pumping his hips and used his hand to stroke Charlie's cock.

"Ahhh! Josh! I'm coming!" Charlie's head thrashed on the bed before a stream of come was pulled from him.

"Fuck!" Josh pumped into Charlie until he had nothing left to unload. He let go of Charlie's cock and braced his other elbow down, bracketing Charlie's head again.

Charlie felt the sticky come between them but didn't care. His eyes leaked from how perfect it had been.

"Charlie?" Josh brushed at his cheeks. "You okay? Did I hurt you?"

Charlie took a breath and smiled. "Fuck, no. When can we do that again?"

Josh paused, then burst out laughing, making Charlie wince when his cock left his ass. "Oh, god! Give me a little recovery time first."

They stayed together for a while before deciding they needed a shower. Josh climbed off Charlie and pulled him up with his hands. As they stood, Josh asked. "Was it okay?"

Charlie wrapped his arms around Josh's head. "The best. Thank you."

20

Charlie

One Year Later

"Yo, Charlie!" He looked up. "You doing any of your demonstrations tonight? I have someone who'd love to see them." Johnson had his arm around a woman, making Charlie arch his eyebrows. Charlie had thought Johnson was gay and had a boyfriend. Anyway, whatever. He might ask Analise about it later.

"I hadn't planned to yet, but I might be able to squeeze one in now." Charlie looked over at Josh and winked. "Hey J, you fancy a demo."

"Hell, yeah!" Josh finished up the drink he was doing, placed it in front of the customer and turned back to Charlie. "Let's go."

Charlie rang the bells, making the customers cheer and shout. Josh flipped the lights and turned on the music. Getting the relevant bottles, glasses and shakers ready, they took position. As the music got going, Charlie tapped the bar four times and off they went.

In unison, they flipped bottles, filled shakers, danced around and laughed. They had been practising this for the past year since the night of the court case to be specific. They laid awake that night talking about everything and Josh had hit on an idea about a cocktail show at the bar.

After talking it over with Tom when they'd gotten home, 'Cocktail Demo' had been born. Every time they were on shift together, they would perform a routine they'd perfected after months of practice. He didn't even want to think about how many bottles and glasses they had broken over all that time.

Since Jimmy, Aiden and Travis had been convicted a year ago, life had gone almost back to normal. People made comments as they were passing by, they were stared at, but eventually, everything had calmed. They were still stared at by people who don't care about the truth, but it was becoming fewer and fewer as time went on. Most people were willing to let the issue go unless it was thrown in their face.

Josh was there to talk him down when it was too much. And Charlie was there when Josh needed it. And if they both did; well, they had their family and friends who had stuck by them to help them out.

His dad and Johnson had given them the best advice though and it was one which, even today, they still listened to—keep talking, don't bottle it up.

And they'd never been happier.

Oh, except when they'd bought their own house together.

Josh had started university last September and was thoroughly enjoying it. He had a few paintings that were in a very small gallery in a town a few miles away. He'd sold one, but the others had not gone yet, but Charlie was sure they would. Family and friends had insisted on buying some of them. There was one, though, that they'd kept for home. It was the one Josh had been painting when they were in the middle of all the hassle from last year. Josh had told him it reminded him of Charlie, so it took centre stage in their front room. And Charlie loved it.

Josh sometimes stayed at the uni if he had a late finish or early start. Otherwise, he'd drive the almost hour-long journey home each night. Every holiday was spent together and the nights tending bar, showing everyone their newfound skills.

Charlie was so happy. He'd never thought he would ever have this, especially with Josh. But look at him now. He must have done something right.

Coming back to the present, Charlie finished off the routine with a flourish amid shouts and clapping. He gave everyone a wave, then turned to Josh and found him on the floor.

Clapping his hand over his mouth, Charlie stared at Josh on one knee, hand held out with an open box in his hand. The whole bar had gone quiet.

"Charlie. You are the best thing ever to happen to me, and I can't imagine my life without you in it. We've been through so much and come out stronger because of it. Will you marry me?"

Charlie cried as he nodded and flung his arms around Josh's neck. Josh pulled back after a moment and took the ring out of the box. Looking into Charlie's eyes, he pushed the ring on his finger and kissed him.

"I love you, Charlie Bear."

"And I love you, J."

"There is something else in there too." Josh released Charlie and pulled a red heart from the box. Holding it up, he turned it so Charlie could see it. In the centre of the heart, were their names. "I thought we could hang it up on the noticeboard. A reminder of where we belong."

Charlie's tears were streaming down his face as he nodded, stumbling along as Josh pulled him towards the end of the bar where the new noticeboard was situated. Letting go of his hand, Josh reached up and attached it to the peg that Charlie was sure hadn't been there earlier.

Once he was done, Josh wrapped his arm around Charlie, resting their heads together as they looked at it.

"One for us, too." Tom attached another heart from the other side of the bar. Inside the heart was Tom and Ginny's names. "A reminder of where we *all* belong."

• • • ● ● • ● ● • • •

Find some more characters from the same world in the Just A Little Crush series. Read on for a teaser of He's Behind You.

And you'll receive a free short story, exclusive content and updates if you sign up to my newsletter.

He's Behind You Teaser

Declan

"**D**eclan! Micah! What the hell are you playing at?" Simon shouted at them. The director usually had a lot of patience, but he had stopped them more times than Declan could count that afternoon. "What the hell happened between last week and now? You both had this down. Why are you fumbling around like newborn foals? If you don't get your heads out of your asses, you'll be out of a job! The performances start tomorrow!" He emphasised the final word before turning around and rubbing his hands over his hair. "Take a break, but I want you back in ten minutes."

Declan hustled to the break area, grabbing a fresh bottle of water and guzzling several mouthfuls. He was fucking exhausted already, but most of it was to do with a tall, slender guy with porcelain skin and red, curly hair. Since their…moment last weekend, Declan had only slept in short bursts, being woken by dreams he didn't want to remember, then unable to sleep for several hours afterwards unless he'd jacked off.

He couldn't help but remember the way Micah smelled, like gingerbread and musk; the sounds Micah made when their tongues twined; the hardness of Micah's cock against his own. Said cock perked up at the images flowing through his brain, and Declan inhaled deeply, trying to focus his thoughts elsewhere.

He knew they needed to discuss it, but Declan was afraid it would make it more real rather than a drunken hazy dream he could pretend didn't happen, even if only in his brain on the odd occasion it switched off.

Micah entered the break room, and Declan threw his empty bottle in the bin and exited, hearing a huff behind him but ignoring it. He strode to the stage, ready—but maybe not quite willing—to go through it again, hopefully without second-guessing where he put his hands while they were dancing.

That was the problem. Before, Declan hadn't had to worry about it because, although Micah was gay, Declan had no reason to think about where his hands went. Micah knew Declan was straight; therefore, he wasn't worried about Micah thinking Declan was trying it on with him. It was only dancing, after all.

Now they'd had...that moment, Declan was concerned Micah would get the wrong idea. He knew it was stupid, but he couldn't help it. So, their dancing had been a mess of fumbling hands and fingers, which was all Declan's fault.

"Right, you two. Are you ready to try again?"

Declan nodded and got into position. This section of the show was where the snowman introduced the boy to Father Christmas. The dialogue was no problem at all, but then the boy stepped away, and the snowman and Father Christmas began a dance before all the other snowmen joined in for the party. They had to bow to each other, hold opposite hands, dance up and down the stage before helping each other to do a kind of air kick around the area. Once they'd done it, they danced a short tango sequence to make the audience laugh before the snowman pushed Father Christmas away and pretended to become shy. That section was more aimed at the grown-ups.

"Well, it was significantly better than what you have been doing today, but it's not up to par compared to last week. What's going on? Have you two had a lover's tiff?" Simon chuckled.

"No!" Declan hissed. "I'm tired, is all."

Simon rubbed his face. "If you're tired after four days of rest, Dec, what are you going to be like by the end of the complete run?" He sighed. "Get some rest. I'd like you back for one more go through in three hours, then we'll let the chips lie where they fall." He turned and walked away.

Declan felt his face get warm as his insecurities about ageing out of the theatre came back to the forefront of his mind.

"Don't you dare," Micah growled, coming to stand in front of Declan. Declan was so surprised, he stayed still. "You are not getting old. Get that thought right out of your head. The theatre keeps you young forever."

Micah gave a half-smile, which Declan returned. Turning to walk away, he felt Micah fall into step beside him.

"Talk to me, Dec. Please."

Declan gritted his teeth, the brief humour they'd shared disappearing. "There's nothing to talk about."

They both entered the changing room, where several people were in the process of changing costumes. Declan was glad their conversation could not be continued, so he grabbed his stuff and left as soon as he was ready. He would have enough time to grab a bite to eat, have a bath and give himself a stern talking to before heading back to the theatre. By that point, he should be back to normal. He hoped.

Grab the book here : https://books2read.com/hesbehindyou

Books by Elouise East

Illuminate Matchmaking
Ignite
Blaze
Kindle
Scorch

Club Royal
Royal Firsts
Rogue Royal
Secretive Royal
Grieving Royal
Disowned Royal
Trained Royal
Awakened Royal
Commanding Royal

Boys, Daddies, Snuggles & More
Need Him
Trust Him

Daddy
Love Me, Daddy
Soothe Me, Daddy

Spoil Me, Daddy
The Complete Daddy Series

Love in Flames
Out of the Frying Pan
Smokescreen
Breathing Fire
Love in Flames Collection

Crush
Love Conquers
Instant Desire
Primary Seduction
Deep Down
A Crush for Christmas
Life Support
Covert Strength
Love Scene
Lawful Attraction
Crush Collection Volume 1
Crush Collection Volume 2
Crush Collection Volume 3

Just A Little Crush
First Kiss
He's Behind You
A Special Love
Three Thirds
Sweet Truths

Standalone
Treehouse Whispers
Star-Crossed

Protecting the Thief
Sizzling Chauffeur

<u>Elouise R East (taboo)</u>
Dark & Divergent
Forbidden Temptation
Too Many Secrets

Collide
When Fantasies Collide
When Dreams Collide
When Pleasures Collide
When Cravings Collide

About Elouise East

E louise East writes sweet and steamy connections in gay romance. She also touches on taboo stories under the name Elouise R East.

Books that tell the stories where friendship and family are the focal point - be it blood family or chosen - are very important to her. That's why she includes a variety of personalities, talents, ages, situations and abilities as she believes a story or character needs. She wants her characters to be real, to be relatable, to be free to have whatever views they tell her they have. And trust her, most of the time, she does not have *any* say in the matter!

Her characters come to life on the page for her as well as her readers. Their stories unfold in front of her as she writes, and she has very little input into how they want to be shown. Just like real life, the lives of her characters change with every choice, every interaction and every conversation. And she wouldn't have it any other way.

She writes books that are emotionally realistic, even if liberties are taken with other aspects of the stories. She doesn't know any other way to write. It comes from deep inside.

Who is she? A single parent to two children living in the UK. An avid reader who still tries to devour every book she can get her hands on. A student of learning about any subject that takes her fancy. An author of books she would read herself. And a romantic at heart who loves anything cheesy.

Who's joining her on her journey?

Stalk her here... ;-)

Website : https://elouiseeast.com

Newsletter : https://elouiseeast.com/newsletter

All links : https://elouiseeast.com/links

www.ingramcontent.com/pod-product-compliance
Lightning Source LLC
Chambersburg PA
CBHW062002190726

48285CB00003BA/882